BROKEN
innocence

BLACKCHAPEL BASTARDS

HALLIE
BENNETT

Did you miss the first book in the Blackchapel Bastards series? Read Whispered Desire—a steamy opposites attract romance—here[1]!

If you read Whispered Desire, make sure you've finished its epilogue[2] to find out how Allie got Pretty Kitty.

---

1. https://www.amazon.com/Whispered-Desire-Romance-Blackchapel-Bastards-ebook/dp/B0DZW3P6CB

2. https://bookhip.com/MKDPBBQ

CONTENT NOTES

Stalking, Kidnapping, DubCon, Toxic Family, Violence, Explicit Sex, Cursing/Offensive Language, Human Trafficking (not hero or heroine), Period Blood Sex, Light Anal, Forced Exhibitionism, Threat of rape (not from hero to heroine)

GLOSSARY

Mamma = Mom

Papà = Dad

Non hai scelta. = You don't have a choice.

Carissima = Dearest

Lo farai, bella ragazza. Non hai scelta. = You will beautiful girl. You have no choice.

Dolce farfalla = Sweet Butterfly

Cristo, presto scoperò quelle tette grosse. = Christ, soon I'm going to fuck those fat tits.

La mia piccola farfalla = My little butterfly

Buonanotte, mia piccola farfalla. Prova a sognarmi, perché io sogno sempre te. = Goodnight, my little butterfly. Try to dream of me, because I'm always dreaming of you.

Mon amour = My love

PREFACE

Once upon a time, seven illegitimate sons of the world's most powerful men arrived at Blackchapel Manor. Young and embittered, the lives they knew were gone forever, to be replaced by one ruthless goal—revenge.

In the thick of the woods, a crumbling stone chapel became their classroom. They didn't learn how to read or write within its cold interior, but to torture and kill those who would compromise their mission to destroy the men who fathered then abandoned them.

Named for the dark deeds conducted inside, seven boys became seven men known as the Blackchapel Bastards.

Mathias Beaumont.

Aleksei and Dmitri Petrov.

Luca D'Amora.

Jonah Anderson.

Hugo Steele.

Rafael Vasquez.

Boys who entered Blackchapel orphaned and unskilled.

Until a brotherhood of men emerged—dangerous and craving retribution.

PROLOGUE

LUCA D'AMORA

TEN YEARS OLD

"*Papà*, I don't want to stay here," I say for the fifth time. My father, Enzo D'Amora, ignores me and uses the hefty door handle to announce our arrival at the manor. Green ivy climbs the brick walls of the massive structure, and I'm reminded of *Mamma's* favorite book, *The Secret Garden*. I wonder if there is one hiding around here, too.

"*Non hai scelta*. With your *mamma* gone, this is the best place for you." Enzo has explained this multiple times, but I still don't understand why I must lose my *Papà* and *mamma* within the same week.

"I'm your son. I should live with you." My arms cross over my chest as I glare stubbornly at the huge oak door that swings open.

A man and a boy my age stand in the entry to greet us.

"Enzo," the man clips, offering his hand to my father.

"Conrad." They nod in greeting before *Papà* tells me to follow the boy. "Hugo will show you to your new room. Remember to behave."

"Listen to your father," Conrad adds with a thread of warning. "Blackchapel Manor is your home now. Don't disrespect it... or me. Hugo!"

The boy hurriedly grabs my arm and tugs me toward the massive staircase that climbs higher into the mysterious manor. He mutters under his breath, "Come on. I'll introduce you to Mathias and Jonah."

There are more boys?

Suddenly, this feels more like an orphanage for the unwanted than a safe haven while *Papà* figures out what to do with me. I know he loves me. He and *Mamma* said so. But he's also part of the Italian mafia and is married to the don's daughter. He can't have a bastard son living with his wife and newborn son—my half-brother.

That's what I overheard him tell *Mamma* the day before she succumbed to her illness.

So, I need to live at Blackchapel Manor with his old friend Conrad Steele until he can figure out other arrangements.

But I'm starting to wonder if *Papà* will come back for me at all...

CHAPTER ONE

EDEN MARINO

PRESENT DAY

My parents warned me about living alone as a single woman. It's dangerous and tough and *not done* by good Italian daughters. Girls belong at home under the protection of their fathers until that responsibility transfers to their husbands through marriage—an old-fashioned belief for a family built on traditions.

But to paraphrase Charlotte Lucas from *Pride & Prejudice*, I'm twenty-eight-years-old with no romantic prospects, which means I could be living with my parents forever.

A scary and wholly unwelcome thought.

That's how I finally gathered enough courage to visit apartment complexes three weeks ago before choosing one, signing the lease, and announcing my plans to move a week later. Thankful that my daycare job covers rent and bills, rather than needing to rely on my dad's support.

Raised in a conservative Italian family that also happens to be part of *The Family*, I was pleasantly surprised when my father agreed to let me leave my childhood home with minimal fuss. If I have to reassure him on every phone call and at every

Sunday dinner that I'm safe, happy, and firm in my decision, it's a small price to pay for independence.

"Remember, you can come home whenever you want to," Dad reminds me for the umpteenth time.

"You'll be the first to know if I change my mind."

Though the likelihood of that happening is nonexistent. My dad is a low-level member of the Italian mafia, so while we've always been on the edges of the organization, it's never been completely forgotten how tenuous our position is. One wrong move on Dad's part, and Don D'Amora could wipe us out.

But in my apartment, it's easy to pretend I'm not part of that life anymore.

Why would a mafia don care about a low-ranking soldier's daughter? Especially one who isn't as glamorous as Alessia Gallo or as influential as Bianca Morelli?

Most of the time, *The Family* forgets my name. Weddings. Funerals. Birthday parties. No one ever remembers Danny Marino's chubby, quiet daughter.

"We're having roast for Sunday dinner. Don't forget to lint roll your clothes before coming over. Last week, your mother couldn't stop sneezing for hours after you left."

"I won't forget. Love you." Our call ends with an electronic beep. I lay the phone face down on the empty cushion beside me and focus on the purring feline in my lap.

Without my mother's allergies to worry about, I had adopted the cat I'd always wanted, yet my parents still try to manage me from afar.

Petting Beanie's orange fur, I sigh and relax into the couch cushions, enjoying the silence while staring at the small stained-glass light catcher hanging by the window, mesmerized by the flash of colors. The butterfly wings twinkle in shades of blue, but the body is an amalgamation of yellows and oranges.

It appeared in my mailbox wrapped in plain brown paper the day after I moved in. A nice surprise that I assumed came from the apartment complex as a welcome gift, although it was strange that they didn't include a note.

Of course, there's a slim chance it was meant for the previous tenant, but...

"Finders keepers. Right, Beanie?"

My new furry friend meows in agreement.

***

"Shoot!" I shake my hand out to alleviate the pain from the kitchen drawer slamming my finger. Growing up in a strict household meant curbing curse words. It's a habit that serves me well at a daycare full of children, but it doesn't quite hit the spot at home.

Shit, I mentally correct myself, practicing one of the New Year's resolutions I made to cuss more as a way to express my feelings rather than bottling them up.

Beanie watches me from her perch on the counter. No matter how many times I've spritzed her with a water bottle to deter her from hopping onto the counters, she refuses to be disciplined. She does what she wants and doesn't care what I think about it.

Honestly, I could probably learn something from the stubborn feline. How to live life on my own terms. How to ignore the things that don't serve my best interests.

Because I care too much about how others view me—a difficult pattern to break when I'm not used to being seen. So, when someone *does* actually notice me? I feel the pressure to be absolutely perfect.

I don't want to be a disappointment.

I need to *earn* their attention.

"God, that's some messed-up thinking, huh?" Beanie blinks in response. "Thanks for the words of encouragement," I joke, scratching under her chin. She may not say much, and she may be a little rebellious terror, but that doesn't stop my obsession with her fluffy butt.

"Okay, let's figure out why the dishwasher isn't working." Leaning against the counter, I skim the pages of the appliance manual I pulled from a bottom drawer. I've been getting by with hand washing the dishes, but I feel stupid for not knowing how to get water to fill the dishwasher, so it's time to figure it out.

The darn—*damn*—thing can't be broken since it's supposed to be new, which means it's a user error. This user just has to learn how to correct whatever I'm doing wrong. Something the manual doesn't help with.

"No worries... This is why the internet was invented." Multiple searches later, though, all the suggestions land me no closer to a working dishwasher, and the next round of potential fixes requires a handyman.

"I'm sure they handle tons of dumb requests," I murmur in a vain attempt to boost my confidence. Spring Falls Apartments has a tab on their website where residents can submit maintenance requests, so it shouldn't be a big deal, but a wave of embarrassment hits me as I fill out the short online form.

Who can't figure out their own dishwasher? It's not freaking—*fucking*—rocket science.

I press the 'submit' button before chickening out.

Most people would probably call their dad or boyfriend to fix the problem, but Danny Marino is not very handy, and we've already established that I'm not the kind of girl who grabs men's attention.

I'm used to being on the sidelines. Overshadowed by the more outspoken, the more beautiful, the more *everything*. And in a huge Italian family like Don D'Amora's branch of the Boston mafia, that's a lot of people.

Leaving the kitchen to settle on the sofa, I open the reading app on my phone. It's times like these—when I'm reminded of how lonely and unseen I feel—that a good old-fashioned romance novel becomes an absolute necessity.

A glimmer of hope in an imaginary world where women like me find true love.

CHAPTER TWO

LUCA

The Blackchapel Bastards.

That's what people call me and my brothers.

We were raised by Conrad Steele to be deadly mercenaries whose goal was the implosion of The Syndicate, the organization that blacklisted Conrad decades ago. Our childhoods were hell, and it shaped each of us into brutal killers, though we don't advertise those skills.

Most of the world recognizes Mathias and myself as the leaders of Blackchapel Incorporated, the legitimate company we run all of our Blackthorn dealings through.

Blackchapel and Blackthorn.

Two sides of the same coin. One is legal and publicly acknowledged, while the other encompasses the dark underbelly of our criminal organization. The angel and devil working together.

As COO of Blackchapel, that puts me firmly on the angel side, but I'm as far as angelic as a man can get.

Evidenced by the latest skills I've added to my dark web resume: *stalker*.

Because I watch sweet and innocent Eden Marino every night. With the curtains open, the bright lights of her apartment serve as a beacon guiding me home. To *her*. My beautiful Butterfly.

9

It's obvious she thinks her place on the third floor of the building protects her from curious eyes, especially when a line of towering trees forms a privacy barrier.

She has no idea a predator stalks her every move, or else she'd be more careful.

Like when she gets out of the shower and traipses around the living room with damp hair and a thin tee fluttering over her curves. Natural. Vulnerable. *No panties.* Sharing glimpses of her bare pussy to my perch on a thick tree branch outside.

Then there was that one glorious time when shadows flashed over her body as my girl felt daring enough to straddle the couch arm and grind against a unique sex pillow while cupping a heavy breast and tweaking the nipple.

Her other hand had pressed against the window glass for stability, and I imagined covering it with mine as I entered her from behind, riding her hard until she came. The cry of her release that day will forever echo in my mind, etching the perfect moment into eternity.

My girl is exploring her newfound freedom. Without the constant hovering of her parents, she's testing her limits, acting brazenly in the safety of her home.

Because she doesn't think anyone can see her.

Doesn't think anyone will know her dirty secrets.

But I do, and I crave more.

***

A notification appears at the top of my screen—an email with a request from Eden to the maintenance team at her apartment complex. Brow wrinkling in disapproval, I open the message to see what the problem is while debating how unhinged it'd be to show up on her doorstep and fix her dishwasher myself.

After all, that's why I installed the spyware on her laptop when she left it unattended at the library months ago. To keep a watchful eye on her. *For her safety.* Not because I'm an obsessed stalker... or not *only* because of that.

And how safe is it to have strange men entering her apartment while she's alone?

"Do you have something to add, Luca?" Mathias asks from the end of the conference table at Blackchapel Incorporated headquarters. I must have made a sound of annoyance for Mathias to call me out.

We're in a meeting with shareholders going over third quarter profits after acquiring Petit Enterprises earlier this year. It's boring as hell, but as CEO and COO, we're both expected to be in attendance.

Too bad my woman takes precedence over everything else.

"I forgot I have an important appointment to attend. Excuse me." I gesture for the marketing exec presenting the financials with one of our accountants to continue before exiting, returning my attention to the issue at hand: another man invading my girl's home.

My assistant scurries down the hall after me. "You don't have an appointment on the schedule, Mr. D'Amora. Did I miss something?" Wallace swipes across his tablet in search of my elusive meeting.

"No, this is a private matter. Cancel the rest of my day," I order before closing the door to my office. The surrounding skyscrapers shoot blinding rays of sunlight through the floor to ceiling windows as I settle behind my desk, rattling the mouse to clear the screensaver of Beanie staring up at the butterfly suncatcher I gifted Eden.

Anyone else who saw the image might wonder at my choice—orange cats don't mesh well with someone known for being part of a group called the Blackchapel Bastards—but I don't give a fuck. It's the closest I can keep Eden without uploading an actual picture of her, and that's a definite *no* until I can ensure her safety in my world.

The seven of us known as the Blackchapel Bastards were raised to exact revenge on our fathers by Conrad Steele. He harbored a deep bitterness after being blackballed. It's what motivated him to take in the illegitimate sons of The Syndicate's most powerful men—some aware of Conrad's actions, like my father when he abandoned me at Blackchapel Manor, and some completely clueless that an enemy trained their bastard child for vengeance.

I doubt my father knew the extent of Conrad's hatred when he dropped me off on his doorstep, especially since the two men were close friends at one point. Sometimes I wonder if Enzo D'Amora had known what was in store for his seven-year-old son, if he'd have made a different choice.

If he'd have kept me.

"Not fucking likely," I scoff under my breath. Enzo had a wife and a new baby. He didn't need the progeny of his dead mistress hanging around to mess up his perfect little life.

Shoving thoughts of my father aside, I open the browser on my computer. Rudimentary knowledge of hacking gets me access to the maintenance team's simple tracking system for requests, so I can mark Eden's submission as completed before some other bastard gets to it, then I hurry to my car and Spring Falls.

The apartment complex is in the suburbs and a bit of a drive from downtown Boston, but it gives me time to listen to a video about dishwashers, glancing at the visual step-by-step instructions every so often. I'm better at killing men than repairing appliances, thanks to a childhood of violence and twisted lessons from Conrad, but murder won't help Eden. A working dishwasher will.

Groups of buildings appear as I pull into the gated complex with Eden's code—another detail learned through computer snooping. This is a new development with all the hallmarks of a wannabe luxury build. Varying shades of gray with wooden accents. A list of amenities including two dog parks, a giant playground, and a clubhouse next to the pool and jacuzzi. It's nice and safe and exactly what I'd choose for Eden while waiting until she can live with me at Blackchapel Manor.

A couple of lawn care guys are mowing the grass and blowing leaves off the sidewalks, their neon green shirts glowing with the company logo.

"Shit." Glancing down at my charcoal slacks and suit jacket, I look as far from a maintenance worker as Pluto is from the sun. No way Eden's going to believe my lie.

Another curse fills the car.

I mentally make a note to acquire the correct maintenance uniform for future visits as my fingers tap a frustrated beat on the steering wheel before landing on a possible solution. There's a gym bag with a change of clothes in the trunk. Athleisure may not say 'handyman,' but casual wear has got to be better than my current attire, right?

"I'm a fucking idiot," I mutter to myself, grateful that none of my brothers-in-arms are here to witness this ridiculous scenario. They'd laugh their asses off at the dilemma I've tossed myself into.

All because of a woman.

Eden's got me all twisted up, and we've never even officially spoken to each other.

Parking at the clubhouse to change in one of the bathrooms, I key in Eden's code again to open the locked door. A man and a woman work on laptops in the corner, too focused on their tasks to acknowledge my arrival.

Good. That means they won't notice when I leave in a totally different outfit. The security cameras will need to be wiped later to erase my presence, but that should be simple enough.

My gaze studies the wrinkled tee skimming over my chest in the bathroom mirror, and I shake my head, reluctantly amused by my predicament.

The things I do for my girl...

CHAPTER THREE

EDEN

"Coming!" Whipping my Rainbow Childcare polo off, I toss it on the bed and reach for a clean tee from my closet.

I had just gotten home from work and started my daily ritual of unwinding from sticky hands and babbling toddlers when someone knocked on my front door.

I don't know who would stop by unannounced.

My parents aren't the type to visit on a whim. Neither are the few friends I have. But clearly, someone needs to talk to me, and I hate making them wait. Even if they're the ones interrupting my evening and not the other way around.

Swinging the door open without hesitation, I begin rambling, slightly out of breath from rushing. "Hi, sorry for the wait! I—" My apology comes to a screeching halt once my brain registers the person standing on my doorstep.

It's a man.

An extremely handsome one—chiseled jaw with dark stubble, piercing blue eyes that promise sin and danger—staring at me like I'm the last piece of cake at a birthday party.

Wait, what?

Blinking away the imagined hunger in his gaze, I brace myself against the door, my nails digging into my palms as I try to regain control of my wayward thoughts.

"Um, can I help you?"

He lifts the small toolbox in his hand. "Maintenance. I'm here to fix your dishwasher."

"Oh!" Stepping back, I wave him inside. "I wasn't expecting you to come so quickly."

"Is it a bad time?" he asks. His gravelly voice scrapes along my nerves, causing a bolt of heat to flare to life under my skin. If I were a different kind of girl, I'd flirt and explore this burst of attraction, especially since my only options for a love life between home and work are service providers who literally show up at my door—solicitors, the UPS guy, *maintenance men*.

But I'm me, and I'm not going to harass a guy who's just doing his job.

"No, you've got perfect timing. I just got home," I say, gesturing toward the kitchen. "The dishwasher is in there. I tried troubleshooting potential issues myself but didn't get far. Hopefully, that's just a *me* problem, and it's still an easy fix."

"Let's find out, shall we?" He sets his tools on the vinyl flooring then crouches down to study the stainless-steel appliance before opening the cabinet doors under the sink. "I'm Luca, by the way."

"Eden." *Obviously.* I mentally slap my forehead. The man knows who I am because he's fulfilling my repair request.

He's got my name, address, and phone number. He's even got *Beanie's* name since the maintenance team asks about pets that may need restraining.

I bite my lip to prevent another embarrassing mishap.

His navy tee strains across his broad shoulders as he ducks lower and fiddles with a few things after starting the dishwasher. It rumbles to life, but the sound of water flowing inside doesn't happen.

"Hmm... I think I've found the prob—Jesus H. Christ!" There's a loud thump as Luca hits his head on the bottom of the sink while Beanie slinks along his exposed legs. Gym shorts as part of a uniform aren't what I would have chosen for a maintenance worker, but I suppose it makes it easier to bend and examine tough spots.

It also provides easy access for curious felines interested in scent marking newcomers.

"Sorry!" Scooping Beanie into my arms, I wince when a pained curse echoes from below. "Beanie has a hard time with boundaries."

"Clearly," Luca grunts, pulling his bruised head from the cabinets. "She skipped the pleasantries and went straight for my dick."

An embarrassed blush rises to my cheeks as my eyes drop to his lap where a long, thick bulge rests across his inner thigh. *Well, damn.* I didn't realize a man's cock could hang that far down his leg. No wonder he freaked. Beanie *was* awful close...

"She didn't mean any h-harm," I stutter, forcing words past my suddenly dry throat and licking my lips.

All while staring at Luca's dick.

What am I doing?

Ding, ding, ding!

Embarrassing Mishap #2.

I may never submit another maintenance request again.

Dragging my gaze away from Luca, it snags on the sofa in front of the living room window, and another flush of heat settles between my thighs at an inconvenient memory.

I was feeling particularly horny and adventurous after reading a sexy romance the other day and rode the couch arm to a wild orgasm, testing out the specially designed pillow I bought for self-pleasuring occasions.

A random ad on social media had intrigued me, and before I knew it, I'd ordered the blasted thing.

Luca cleared his throat and sat up with a groan. "It's fine. At least your dishwasher is working properly now."

The swish of water drowns out the awkward moment, and I sigh in relief. "Thank you so much! What was the problem?"

"When it was installed, they didn't turn the water back on once the piping was hooked up. I just needed to turn the little knob back there." He points to a silver ring toward the back of the sink cabinet.

"Oh, so it *was* a simple fix." God, I should have been able to figure that out. "Sorry for wasting your time."

"Don't apologize." Luca stands in a mesmerizing display of shifting muscles until he towers above me, my head craning back to maintain eye contact with his face rather than his impressive... *package*. "There's a system to input maintenance requests for a reason. I'll always come when you need me."

The intensity in his rough-hewn features sets off a flurry of butterflies in my stomach. His seriousness should be a red flag. We're talking about replacing air filters or fixing leaky faucets, but for some reason, my only concern is not appearing as dumb as I feel.

"Well, I appreciate your patience. I promise not to bother you unless it's an emergency. Same goes for any of your team members assigned to my case first."

"That won't happen," he growls. My teeth catch on my bottom lip to hide a pleased smile until he coughs into his fist and recovers. "I mean, this building is my responsibility, so it'll always be me."

Tomato red is not my color, but that doesn't stop the flush on my skin from deepening in self-recrimination. Of course, the complex assigns their maintenance workers to zones. That's a logical way to keep everyone organized. My reading into Luca's immediate denial of anyone else helping me except for him is a result of too many nights staying up late to finish my beloved romance novels.

All those alpha heroes have warped my brain if I'm imagining this guy, *who is just doing his job*, being interested in seeing me again for more than professional reasons.

"Right. Thank you again," I say too brightly, walking him out once he's gathered his toolbox. As soon as he's gone, I slump forward and bang my forehead on the closed door.

But I don't have too long to wallow in self-recrimination because another knock rattles the doorframe.

"What is going on today?" I rarely get visitors, and now two in one day?

Please don't be Luca.

My poor body can't take another encounter with the hot maintenance man so soon after flustering through this last visit. However, instead of a man, there's a cardboard box that greets me, my name scrawled across the side.

"What do you think it is?" I ask Beanie as she rubs against the box edge after I drag it inside. Tearing off the tape at its sides, I unfold the top flaps to reveal a foam box housing an elaborate bouquet of chocolate-covered fruit. Cool air wafts from the chilled container as I reach inside. The attached card lists multiple fruits and a variety of chocolates.

It's an extravagant arrangement, and frankly, I'm not sure how I'm going to eat all of this before it goes bad, but I'm sure going to try because this probably cost a fortune.

"This must be the final gift. The grand finale to the Spring Falls welcome campaign."

Beanie doesn't respond except to start chewing on the plastic cellophane wrapped around the bouquet. Obviously, I'm not the only one who thinks the new arrival looks delicious.

Unraveling the ribbon tied around the top, I pull the plastic back far enough to grab a skewer with a pretty pineapple star half-dipped in chocolate. The first bite is a juicy combination of sweet fruit and bitter dark chocolate, and a hum of pleasure sticks in my throat.

When I researched apartments, I pored over online reviews to avoid getting into a bad situation, especially since my parents' warnings constantly whispered in the back of my mind. Spring Falls had high ratings and all the amenities I was looking for, but no one mentioned how generous a company they were.

Every few days, a surprise gift has awaited me either in my mailbox or the welcome mat in front of my door. First, the butterfly light catcher arrived. Next, potted tulips, which are my favorite flowers.

Then came a book of recipes for healthy cat snacks.

That one caught me off guard because my browser history is filled with cat recipe sites, and it felt a little too *big brother is watching*. But I shrugged off the unease and chalked it up to Spring Falls being extra thorough by gifting items specifically tailored to tenants' needs. I'm sure the dog owners around here received similar books.

But this last gift...

This is beyond generous, and I'll miss the surprises.

While each present was unexpected, they were proof that someone was thinking of me—even if it was a random leasing agent.

Someone thought of Eden Marino. The perpetually overlooked and forgotten. And it was a nice feeling. One I don't get to experience often.

My shoulders deflate. "Guess we better savor this, huh?"

Beanie continues to gnaw at the wrapper in complete agreement.

CHAPTER FOUR

LUCA

"Where's the food, man?" Rafe drops onto the bar stool in front of where I'm preparing a sandwich for dinner. Despite the bad memories imbued in Blackchapel Manor, the seven of us—me, Mathias, Jonah, Dmitri, Aleksei, Rafael, and Hugo—decided to stay here and make it our home and headquarters after Conrad died. Maybe we should have razed it to the ground, but it's part of our history.

And as men with clipped roots, any connection is better than nothing. Even if it is an old brick manor that used to serve as more of a prison than a home.

Lifting a wry brow, I gesture around the kitchen. "Look around. I'm sure you'll find it."

Rafe shakes his head. In desperate need of a trim, the wavy strands of hair fall over his eyes. "Nah, I'm talking about the fruit arrangement you ordered. When is it being delivered? I'm looking forward to those chocolate-dipped pineapple daisies."

"What the hell are pineapple daisies? And how do you know my purchase history? Are you snooping through our bank accounts again?" *Fucking hackers.* Rafael is a whiz on the computer, and he's excellent at finding information we may need in our quest to bring down The Syndicate, but he needs to learn some fucking boundaries.

"I didn't have to snoop. You left the tab open with the confirmation order on the study's shared computer."

Damn it. I'd been too eager to see Eden's reaction to the book of cat recipes set to arrive later that day to go through the usual steps of deleting evidence of my actions. Her excitement while flipping through the pages had been worth the oversight, though. It matched the look of pure joy on her face when she'd discovered the fruit basket earlier this afternoon.

That had been a close call.

After fixing her dishwasher, I'd had to run to my usual hiding spot in the trees once I saw the delivery guy park his van in front of her building.

"If you want pineapple daisies, buy them yourself. That order won't be arriving here anytime soon."

"What he means is that it was already delivered to his girl." Jonah enters the kitchen with Mathias and Allie in tow. The two lovebirds are even more inseparable since they got engaged.

"Luca's got a girl? Since when?" Mathias asks, plucking two slices of turkey from the container and sharing one with Allie. It still surprises me to see Mathias—the Blackchapel Bastards' unofficial leader—so relaxed.

I had my doubts when he brought Allie to stay at the manor all those months ago, especially when I couldn't do the same thing with Eden. *Too risky. Dangerous.* That's what I told myself.

And Allie and Mathias faced their fair share of life-threatening events.

But they made it through. Are engaged. Happy as hell.

My jaw clicks with the grinding of my teeth. *God, I'm so fucking jealous.* I wanted to eat in peace before whiling away the hours until I could visit Eden again tonight.

Instead, I'm faced with what I don't have—my girl at my side—and a family intent on prying into my secrets.

Jonah pretends to think for a minute before snapping his fingers. "Since D'Amora's sixty-fifth birthday celebration. After that, Luca started disappearing most nights." As the head of security for Blackchapel Inc. and its criminal counterpart Blackthorn, it's no surprise Jonah has noticed my regular disappearances. "I assume it has to do with a woman."

Allie's eyes widened in excitement behind her glasses. "You met someone at your dad's party? Who is she?"

"No one." My gut clenches. I hate referring to Eden in that way, because she's far from nothing to me, but I'm not about to launch into an explanation about my personal affairs. I don't care if this is my family. A man's got to have some secrets. "I mean, there isn't anyone. Jonah has too much time on his hands and is pulling stuff out of his ass. Shouldn't you be tailing that journalist and finding out more of what she knows about your dad?"

"Yeah, how is Valerie? Recovered from her run-in with an assassination attempt? Or did she let it scare her off? It's been months since she started that article." Rafe steals a turkey slice for himself, and I give up on having a peaceful meal, shoving the container closer to the group gathered on the other side of the kitchen island.

"She's a professional. Of course, she didn't let Anderson's goons silence her," Jonah says defensively. "She's just been busy with other stories, thanks to her editor."

"Maybe we should invite her to the manor," Allie suggests. "Now that she's met us, she might be more inclined to come here versus a public space. We can see if there's any way we can help expedite things for her."

"Good idea, *mon amour*." Mathias kisses the top of Allie's head as the conversation continues without me, my mind circling back to Eden.

Our lives are dangerous. We're working to dismantle a decades-old crime establishment to ruin the men who abandoned us as boys. That doesn't leave much room for love and relationships.

But somehow Mathias is making it work.

It gives me hope that maybe I won't have to keep my distance from my woman for much longer.

CHAPTER FIVE

EDEN

Dad wipes his mouth with a napkin before tossing it on the dining table and clearing his throat. A silent conversation passes between him and Mom, their eyes speaking a language only couples married for decades know.

"Is something wrong?" I venture, curious about the sudden weight in the air.

Our Sunday dinner was the usual fare of good food and catching up on family news while avoiding the two topics that always cause a strain between us—Dad's off-limits work and my decision to become more independent.

"Far from it," Dad begins as Mom squeezes his hand with a smile. "Don D'Amora called yesterday."

"Are you getting promoted?" Despite my father's age, he's not even a capo in the D'Amora organization, and while I'd hate for him to climb ranks to a more dangerous position, I know receiving praise and recognition from the don is important to him.

"He wanted to discuss you, Eden."

The roast and potatoes I scarfed down meld into a lead pit in my stomach. There's only one reason why an Italian don would talk to a man about his daughter. A trembling hand falls to my belly to curb the nausea threatening to rise.

"Fabian met with his father to relay his interest in you," Dad continues. "As you may know, Fabian is a bit of a womanizer. The don's had his hands full trying to keep the boy on the right path. He's hopeful with this sudden urge to settle down, Fabian might be making a change. Obviously, you're not who Don D'Amora would have originally chosen to marry his son, since our family doesn't come with powerful connections, but the don is willing to overlook that flaw as long as his son is happy."

Did I say *The Family* would forget me?

Never think of me again now that I don't live at home?

Because I was dead wrong.

Somehow, I landed on Fabian D'Amora's radar. *Me.* A woman with no political advantages. A woman he's never spoken to. I'm not even sure how he knew my name to bring it up in a marriage discussion with his father.

"When your father told me, I almost fainted from joy!" No surprise Mom approves of this union.

Me, less so.

I might actually throw up on her favorite Aubusson rug.

"Something isn't right. Why would Fabian want me? We bring nothing to the D'Amoras." I sip at my glass of water, praying hydrating might help cool the sauna the room has turned into. Unfortunately, the liquid sloshes around my belly, making me feel worse.

"We're a loyal Italian family who's never broken the don's trust. For decades, the Marino name has stood for loyalty and devotion—difficult qualities to find in our volatile world," she says, glancing at Dad over their empty plates. "Stop questioning our good fortune and accept your elevated station. You'll be married to the next don!"

From the edges of *The Family* to the very center.
How the *hell* did this happen?

CHAPTER SIX

LUCA

My girl needs me.

Earlier, I caught her crying for the second day in a row as she sat outside on the screened-in patio with her arms curled around her knees and a blanket covering her from head to toe. She wiped her cheeks multiple times while tears fell, and it took all of my strength to resist scaling the building and pulling Eden into my arms.

I'd care for her, give her whatever she needs before finding what *or who* made her cry and dealing with the problem.

Because no one hurts what's mine.

But I forced myself to wait.

Restrained the primal need to shield her from pain because nothing has changed on my end. We're still in the midst of figuring out how to destroy my father and by extension, part of The Syndicate.

That doesn't mean I'm above sneaking a little closer to my Butterfly to make sure she's okay.

The midnight hour casts long shadows as I climb the post leading to her third-story patio. My pocket knife cuts through the mesh screen, and I make a note to fix it later before climbing in and walking to the door leading to her living room. The knob turns easily in my palm.

That won't happen again.

I vow that a lot more security will be added, and this door will remain locked. No one else will be able to get to my Butterfly.

Carpet hushes my footsteps as I step inside her apartment for the second time. It smells like she does: sweet with notes of earthy cinnamon.

Wide eyes stare at me as I pause in front of Beanie. The feline sits stock still like a stone statue rather than a living, breathing being. Lowering to my haunches, I remove the tiny bag of cat treats from my back pocket and shake the contents. Immediately, the furry beast trots closer, purring up a storm while I offer brown bits of kibble.

Bribery works on humans and animals alike it seems.

Once the treats are gone, I head down the hallway to the open bedroom door, inhaling deeply of Eden's addicting scent before stopping beside her bed. Two fans blow on either side of the mattress, causing her blonde waves to flutter in the wind, and the constant roar masks anything but the loudest of sounds.

Not that I make any.

I'm not an amateur when it comes to breaking and entering, although this is my first time slipping into a woman's home for my own selfish reasons.

Removing my leather gloves, I run my bare fingers over her round cheek, a shiver of awareness working through me. To touch her is fucking heaven. My cock hardens with each light stroke, my mind and body fascinated by the innocence radiating from Eden's sleeping form.

I don't want to scare her, and a stranger in her bedroom would surely do so. Which means this is as far as things go tonight, unfortunately.

Soon, sweet Butterfly.

Soon, you'll be mine.

***

"Congratulate your half-brother, Luca. Fabian is finally becoming a man." My father pats Fabian's shoulder as he raises his glass of bourbon in his elegant Beacon Hill brownstone, and I join the toast while maintaining a facade of complete apathy.

Fabian and I aren't close.

He's the legitimate heir to *The Family*.

I'm the illegitimate bastard, borne from our father's past indiscretion.

None of that would matter, though, if Fabian wasn't the world's greatest prick.

"Thank you, Father. I'm sure Luca is overjoyed to see me so happy. Eden Marino will be a sweet little bride, won't she, brother?"

Oh, yeah, and this jackass got himself engaged to my woman.

I don't know why Fabian took an interest in Eden when his usual type is rail thin with fangs for teeth, but the why isn't important when this wedding is never going to happen.

Not while I've still got breath in my lungs.

Enzo wants Fabian married in the hopes that he stops being a damn nuisance by drawing police attention to himself. The cops are in the mafia's pocket, but that doesn't give Fabian a free pass for reckless driving, drug possession, and drunken brawls, though he likes to think so.

There's not a chance in hell Fabian will calm down with Eden as his wife, so maybe I can steer our father in a different direction.

"I don't know her, but Eden sounds like a good woman. Her family isn't very well-connected, though. I'm surprised you approved of the union."

"Fabian made a compelling case." Enzo beams at his younger son whose satisfied smirk grates on my nerves. No way in hell is he getting anywhere near my Eden.

"Let me offer another one," I say, and immediately, Fabian straightens in his seat to glare daggers at me. *Just wait, brother.* "You've been wanting a stronger connection with Blackthorn. Perhaps we've overlooked a simple solution: I could marry someone in *The Family*. Eden, for example. Which would leave Fabian open for a more advantageous match."

Enzo strokes his chin in consideration. "I thought you despised how the mafia forges contracts. You're willing to marry a stranger to strengthen our bond? Your brother's betrothed?"

"Father..."

"Silence," Enzo barks, and Fabian shuts his mouth like the weak little runt he is.

"It's a win-win situation. Eden's family isn't so high in the ranks that people would chafe at her marrying outside the Boston faction, but she's still connected to it. And while I admire my brother's interest in matrimony to a nobody..." I hide my wince at the description. "This isn't the first scheme he's cooked up to get in your good graces after a spot of trouble. I heard about the DUI charge that was dropped last week. I'm guessing his sudden rush to marry a good Italian girl is for your benefit alone. But why go along with a woman of his choosing when it makes sense for Fabian to make a stronger match?"

"You bastard! You..."

"What did I say, Fabian? Your don is speaking, and you will hold your tongue unless you want me to rip it out." The fatherly indulgence that blanketed Enzo before is gone, replaced by the authority of a powerful mafia don. "You make valid points, Luca. I will think about it. Until then, I'll let Marino and his family continue to prepare for a wedding. We won't tell them there might be a change in the groom yet."

Hiding a grin behind my tumbler, I mentally pat myself on the back.

Score: Luca 1. Fabian 0.

Ever since my father's wife died, he's stopped pretending I don't exist. The first overture was an invitation to his birthday party—the one where I saw Eden for the first time. Then he invited me for drinks at his private club where he officially introduced his two sons to each other.

The change in tune—from hiring a crew to kill me in a drive-by shooting in Paris months ago to welcoming me back into the *The Family* fold—raised several red flags, but like the old adage says: *Keep your friends close and your enemies closer.*

Murderous family members included.

I don't know what Enzo's endgame is. Maybe he truly wants to reconnect with the son he abandoned. Maybe this is all an elaborate ruse to secure an alliance with Blackthorn.

At this point, it doesn't matter.

His time's almost up.

And my top priority now is protecting Eden from my asshole half-brother by any means necessary.

CHAPTER SEVEN

EDEN

Day four since my life was blown to smithereens.

I cried Sunday night.

Then again Monday and last night.

All the tears and worrying about my future must have screwed with my brain, too, because I dreamed of a mystery man coming to my rescue. The fantasy breached so far into reality that it felt like he was in my room, stroking my cheek, and comforting me with his protective presence.

If only.

"Damian, pull your pants up, please!" I call to the toddler with his navy joggers around his ankles. I don't know what it is with little boys wanting to get naked whenever and wherever they can, but it's a constant battle between us daycare providers and our male charges.

"I swear these kids are aging me before my time," Corey grumbles good-naturedly. At twenty-two, she's fresh from college and my boss's niece. She's still learning how to balance the two sides of Rainbow Childcare—the helpless babies who hang out in the nursery and the wilder toddlers who rule the playroom.

"Try a different perspective," I tease, dabbing at the smears of paint Raya left on my work polo. "Instead of aging you, they're keeping you young at heart. All that energy can be contagious if you let it."

Corey's expression turns contemplative before a crying match between two girls tugging on opposite ends of a stuffed dolphin toy distracts her. Her aunt and owner of Rainbow Childcare heads that way to calm the girls, and we both watch as one dolphin toy miraculously becomes a pair.

"We'll see..." Corey drawls, then smiles. "But thanks for the advice. How are you doing?"

"What do you mean?"

"You've seemed off this week." She shrugs. "I don't mean to pry, but it looked like you were crying Monday morning."

Crap. I didn't think anybody had noticed the puffiness around my eyes. I'd been careful to splash cold water on my overheated face. Throwing the wet paper towel I'd been using on my shirt in the trash, my mind races for an acceptable excuse to explain what's wrong.

It's not like I can blurt out that I'm being married off to a mafia man.

That would raise all sorts of red flags.

"Just family stuff." The lame reason is close enough to the truth that I don't feel completely awful for lying to her. "I'll be okay, though."

"Are you sure? If you ever want to talk, I'm here for you." Corey squeezes my bicep then adds a quick goodbye when her aunt calls her name.

As kind as the offer is, I won't be confiding in Corey anytime soon. It's safer to keep my personal life separate from my professional, especially now that I've failed to distance myself from *The Family.*

Besides, Corey can't help me.

No one can.

I'm on my own.

***

"Stand straight. We need to get proper measurements for the wedding dress." My mom circles the round platform I'm standing on while the seamstress calls out numbers to her assistant.

Never underestimate a mother eager to marry off her daughter.

Somehow, she landed an appointment with one of Boston's exclusive wedding dress designers, requiring me to drive straight here from work for this impromptu measurements session. Which is exactly what I wanted to do after a day of dealing with dozens of active children.

A dress fitting seems premature given I still haven't officially met my husband-to-be, but Mom and Dad were adamant that the don wants a quick wedding. No waiting and planning an elaborate ceremony over the course of a year. No engagement party. No bridal shower.

I know this marriage is a business transaction rather than a love match, but skipping all the usual wedding prep and events pinches a nerve. I've never been the center of attention. I've always been hidden in the background. Unseen. Unnoticed.

But a woman's wedding?

That's supposed to be her moment to shine, yet I'm once again relegated to a set piece being directed and moved by Don D'Amora and my parents. None of this is for me.

"Is this really necessary? Fabian isn't known for his commitments. He'll probably change his mind about marrying me soon." I cross my fingers, though it's a vain hope.

Marriage contracts are a respected tradition in Italian mob families. You can't just break an engagement. But perhaps a don's son has a little more leeway? He definitely has more power.

I've got no say at all in my future unless I want to run away from everything I've ever known.

The lack of control I have over who I marry is still on my mind hours later as I walk back to my apartment after checking my mail. Distracted, it takes a couple of minutes to register the eerie quiet surrounding me instead of car doors shutting or neighbors walking their dogs.

Quickening my step, I shelf my worries about becoming Fabian's wife and focus on getting home safely. Every scary story my parents told to dissuade me from leaving my childhood home flashes to life as I hurry home from the resident mailboxes.

The walk isn't long, and the sidewalk is well-lit, but I can't shake the feeling of being watched. This isn't the first time I've felt the sensation, but it *is* the first time it's freaking me out so much.

My keys jingle as I arrange them between my knuckles. I've made this journey a dozen times and never felt concerned for my safety. This isn't a neighborhood known for trouble, but something feels off tonight.

You're probably on edge because of the impending nuptials to a complete stranger.

Marrying Fabian D'Amora will put me in the thick of danger, a place I never wanted to be.

Could rival gangs already be planning to use me against him and his father? Against *The Family*?

I'm about to scold myself for how ridiculous that sounds when there's a rustling of leaves to my right. Probably a squirrel, but my pace increases anyway. The entry to my apartment is close, a mere ten feet away, when two bulky arms wrap around my chest and haul me backward.

Mail flutters in the air. My keys clatter to the sidewalk. A yelp of fear bursts from me before my attacker stuffs a ball of cloth in my mouth. The metallic flavor stings my tongue as a second man steps forward and lands a backhand to my cheek.

"This is a mafia princess?" The man behind me scoffs.

"More like her fat servant," his accomplice jokes with a swift punch to my stomach. I groan at the impact. My chin dips low before Thug #2 wrenches my head back by yanking my hair. "Uh-uh, Miss Marino. A couple more bruises, then we'll be done. Courtesy of Fabian's half-brother."

Half-brother?

There have been whispers of Enzo's past indiscretions with a mistress leading to a bastard child, but it wasn't until recently that the rumors were confirmed when the man was invited to Enzo's birthday celebration.

Despite attending the party with my parents, I never met him. I was too busy reading on my phone at an empty table by the exit.

"He thinks he can fuck Fabian over without consequences. Like he's the next in line to become don. Luca needs to be taught a lesson, and unfortunately, you're it."

Luca. The image of my strong and handsome maintenance man ripples into memory. I could use a strong protector right about now.

Because if I'm understanding correctly, my fiancé is the one who arranged for this attack. Because of an illegitimate half-brother.

Somehow, I've fallen into the middle of their sibling rivalry.

"P... Please..." The garbled plea gets lost in the rough cloth filling my swollen cheeks.

Not that it matters.

Both men are focused on their task. They're not even concerned about being caught by my neighbors based on our location between two vehicles. Sure, we're in the shadows, but anyone could walk by.

These men couldn't care less.

"Last one," Thug #2 says as if he's doing me a favor.

After another hit to my ribs, I'm dragged backwards—my head covered with a black hood while my hands are zip tied behind my back—and unceremoniously tossed into a van. My head thumps against the floorboard as my shoulder jambs into something soft. *Another person.* Fear freezes every muscle except for my racing heart.

Where are they taking me?

Why not dump me on the sidewalk?

Who else have they kidnapped?

Frantic questions fill my thoughts as the vehicle rumbles to life. The hood blocks out the light, but it's obvious we're driving away from Spring Falls. I carefully test my bonds and wince at how tightly I'm trussed up.

Rolling toward the stranger next to me, I whisper, "Hello? Can you hear me?"

No response.

Shoot. *Shit.* This definitely calls for cursing.

Ducking my head, I try to maneuver the hood higher to increase visibility, but all I can see are my companion's hands bound like mine, a jade bead bracelet with a *Q* charm on one wrist.

"Are you alright? Please—" The van zooms over a speed bump, or an unlucky animal crossing the road. Either way, the result is the same.

My body flies up then slams down hard enough to halt my cautious attempts at connecting with my companion as a heavy darkness descends on my consciousness.

The last thing to register is the misplaced scent of eucalyptus.

CHAPTER EIGHT

LUCA

Muted conversations carry over the traditional Irish music playing in the background of Delaney's. Blackthorn owns the bar, and we conduct a lot of business here, so I figured it'd be a good spot to start sharing the news of my upcoming nuptials with my brothers.

Enzo hasn't officially approved my proposition, but he will.

He's a smart man. You don't rise to become don of an Italian mob without the brains to back up your brawn—AKA the army of soldiers inherited from your predecessor.

"Let's play a game of pool. You owe me a rematch." Hugo, Rafe, and I head toward one of three billiards tables and wait for the current game to finish before the guys take a hint and leave the table to us. Jonah and Mathias couldn't make it tonight, and Dmitri is off doing Blackthorn business.

"I can't help it if you haven't figured out how the game works yet. It's all about angles. Once you understand that basic principle, maybe you'll stand a chance at beating me," I say.

Rafe racks the balls while Hugo smirks, leaning against the wall to quietly watch our match. He never says much. A result of being Conrad Steele's son, I suppose. While every Blackchapel Bastard had an absent father growing up, Hugo's dad was very much present. Though the murder lessons wouldn't win him any Father of the Year awards.

"I understand the basics, asshole. I just can't visualize a fucking protractor on the table so every shot is the exact right degree like you."

"Yet you still put money on the line thinking you can beat me."

"One of these days it'll happen," Rafe grumbles. The balls scatter across the green bombazine with the crack of the cue ball. Two striped balls drop into side pockets.

"He's playing the long game, Luca," Hugo says, studying the table as Rafe circles it while calculating his next move. "Waiting to hustle you years down the road when you let your guard down."

I chuckle. "Can't wait. We'll be eighty, and Rafe will finally decide to make his move. A plan decades in the making."

"You laugh, but it could happen," Rafe mutters. His shot goes wide, and I grin at the opening.

"Tough luck, kid." Rafe's not that much younger than me, but as the youngest of us, he gets the little brother treatment. Chalking my cue stick, I start calling my shots and clearing the table. "So, I've got some news. I'm getting married."

"What? Since when?"

"To whom?"

After sinking the eight ball, I hand the cue to Hugo, so he can take on Rafe in a more even match. "Eden Marino. I made a deal with Enzo to bring Blackthorn and *The Family* closer."

"Why?" Rafe asks. "We're already working on bringing your dad down. Marrying a stranger isn't necessary."

"Maybe not." I don't tell them that it's *absolutely* necessary for me to marry Eden instead of another man, especially my half-brother. "But it can only help our cause. Enzo will trust me more with another tie to him because this one will be legitimate. There's a mark against me for being his bastard son, but tying myself in a legally binding contract to one of the mafia families kind of balances that out."

I just made that up, but it sounds right.

"And you decided to do this without any input from us?" Hugo asks, his narrowed gaze glancing at me before dropping back to the billiards table. "We're a team. A brotherhood. We can't go off half-cocked when it affects all of us. This Eden woman will surely be asked to spy on us. We'll have to be extra careful with what we discuss around her."

"Eden can be trusted," I grit out. Enzo may ask her to report what she sees at Blackchapel Manor, and she may even agree since he's the don, but I doubt she'll actually follow through, especially once I make it clear that she's safe with me. Fallout from not following the don's orders will never reach her.

"Wait a minute." Rafe straightens and shoots a curious stare my way. "Is this the woman Jonah mentioned? The one you met at Enzo's birthday party? The one you've been stalking most nights?"

"Are you following me?"

"No, but you just confirmed I'm right." He smirks. "Damn, first Mathias and now you. And Jonah's got that journalist. What the fuck is happening to us?"

I don't get a chance to answer when the front door to Delaney's bursts open causing everyone to stare in shocked silence as a newcomer saunters inside. He pauses a second to survey the room before locking eyes with me and striding forward. His companion follows behind, and that's when I notice a hooded woman hanging limply in his arms.

What the fuck?

"A message," the leader says as his buddy dumps the unconscious woman on the billiards table. Pinned to her torn shirt are words that have me seeing red.

You want the bitch? She's yours.

Nausea climbs my throat as I rip the black covering off, and my fears are confirmed.

It's Eden.

Beaten black and blue with trails of blood dried on her chin from a cut lip.

When I look up to interrogate the men who brought her, they're already gone. Probably realized they're dead once I get my hands on them.

"Please tell me this isn't who I think it is." Rafe is rapidly texting on his phone. Most likely a message to notify Jonah, Mathias, and Dmitri of this newest development.

"It is." Carefully scooping Eden into my arms, I forge a path through the stunned crowd of bar patrons. "Call the doctor and have him meet us at the manor."

Fabian's a dead man.

His name was already on my list, right after Enzo's, but now the timeline has been accelerated. My brothers and I will take down Enzo's empire, but Fabian? He's going down much earlier.

Because no one touches my woman and lives to tell about it.

CHAPTER NINE

EDEN

The first thing I notice is the comforting purr of Beanie.

The second is the throbbing ache concentrated around my face and stomach.

Flashes of memories break through the haze of confusion and soreness blanketing me, and my eyes shoot wide open, darting around my elegant surroundings. A canopy of scarlet velvet drapes over the four-poster bed, complementing the heavy wooden furniture tastefully arranged around the room.

Where am I?

This isn't my apartment, yet Beanie's incessant purring isn't my imagination—her chunky weight sits on my chest, a familiar comfort.

A jade bracelet. Eucalyptus. The rattle of an old van.

Someone mentioned a half-brother to Fabian, then... *What?* My head pounds, begging me to stop pushing, but I can't stop. I'm in a strange place with no clue as to how I got here.

A girl's cry.

The memory sharpens for a second before disappearing. Maybe it was my own cry? I study the top of the canopy above me as Beanie's soft fur pushes between my fingers with each slow pet. Footsteps near the room before pausing outside the door.

Both Beanie and I freeze, our heads jerking toward the sound in anticipation, although my cat appears less scared than curious, judging by her sheathed claws and the fact she doesn't immediately scramble for a hiding spot.

The brass knob turns to let in the handsomest man I've ever seen. *And a familiar one.* Broad shoulders stretch the fabric of Luca's ash gray button-down shirt which is tucked into charcoal slacks that skim a sturdy waist and even sturdier-looking thighs.

"Eden..." He breathes my name like it's meant to be whispered in awe. A tray of delicate china rests in his hands, tanned fingers wrapped around the side handles. Saucers clink together as he steps closer, though the kettle and teacup remain still. "How are you feeling?"

Why is my maintenance guy bringing me tea in bed?

Where the heck are we?

Struggling to a less vulnerable position, I sit up and dislodge Beanie, who saunters to the bottom of the bed and offers her head to Luca, her orange tail flicking back and forth.

"Hey, cutie. Are you looking after our girl?" He balances the tray in one arm to free a hand and run it over my traitorous cat's back.

Beanie is a rescue. She lived in the shelter for months before I adopted her from a terrible hoarding situation. The shelter volunteers warned that it took time for her to warm up to people, yet here she is, sidling up to her kidnapper.

Because that's what Luca is, or how else would Beanie be here instead of safe at home sleeping in her favorite cardboard box? Sure, Beanie met him once before—and caused an awkward ending to his visit—but still. This situation calls for caution, not cuddling with a man who, apparently, is a lot more than your average maintenance man.

"What are you doing here, Luca? What am *I* doing here?" My voice croaks out like a bullfrog preparing for a night of annoying his swamp neighbors, and I swallow the little bit of moisture in my mouth to alleviate the dryness. A futile attempt since my tongue and cheeks are currently the Sahara freaking Desert.

"Shh... Don't try to speak yet. Drink this first." He pours a steaming arc of tea into a cup, stirs in a teaspoon of sugar, honey, and cream, then offers the concoction by raising it to my chapped lips. "Your hands are a little banged up," he says by way of explanation.

Ignoring the shiver his soft words provoke, I carefully wrap a hand around the fragile base—the red lashes on my wrists from the zip ties used to bind me a stark contrast to the white ceramic—and take the cup from him. "They're fine. I can handle a tiny teacup."

White teeth shine through the shadow of his beard as a small grin appears. "Of course, you can, Butterfly. How are you feeling? Dr. Bellamy examined you last night, then left a bottle of painkillers."

"I feel like I got run over by a truck." Hot tea isn't usually my go-to, but I can't deny the calming effect the honey and chamomile have as I sip from the delicate gold rim. "Who's Dr. Bellamy? Who are *you*? What's going on?" My voice cracks on the last question, vocal cords straining from overuse.

His weight depresses the mattress beside me, and I work not to dip toward him. He rubs a hand over his bearded cheek before sighing. "Dr. Bellamy is someone we trust to make house calls, and you know who I am except for my last name. I'm Luca D'Amora. What do you remember about last night?"

Luca *D'Amora.*

Fabian's half-brother!

If I squint, the barest of resemblance becomes clear, but for the most part, I never would have guessed they were related. Luca is taller, broader, and infinitely more attractive than Fabian, based on the social media photos I found, though my opinion may be biased considering Luca hasn't had me viciously attacked.

"I was ambushed then tossed into a van by two thugs blaming you for my predicament. Something about payback for Fabian?" A shudder travels down my spine. "They're responsible for this." I nod toward my bruised body.

The muscles of his jaw flex as anger flares in his eyes. "I'm going to kill that motherfucker," he growls under his breath. Clearly, there's no love lost between the two siblings.

But how did I get in the middle of their feud?

I'm engaged to marry Fabian. If someone wanted to exact their revenge through me, shouldn't it have been Luca instead of the other way around?

"How were they able to kidnap you? I went to your apartment to grab Beanie, but it didn't look like the door had been broken in. Was it through the patio?"

"No, I was walking back from the apartment mailboxes. They grabbed me in the parking lot," I murmur, digesting everything he just said. Luca remembered my patio and Beanie from his lone visit to my apartment. Enough to bring my cat here, so she wouldn't be alone.

Because he's not really a maintenance man! Who knows how long he's been watching you?

The teacup trembles in my hand as I consider my options. I really don't want to be a captive again, even if these are much nicer digs than the creeper van where I was held, but I'm hardly fit to escape.

My limbs ache, there's a piercing pain in my temples, and judging by the sunlit window to my right, we're not on the first floor, which means I'd potentially need to navigate a labyrinth of halls for an exit. Frankly, it sounds exhausting just thinking about it.

When I wished to be seen—to not be a faded wallflower in the background—this wasn't what I had in mind: caught between two dubious men in the middle of a power struggle. I dreamed of princes and knights, not freaking villains.

"You shouldn't be walking alone at night, Butterfly. It's not safe."

"Are you blaming me for what happened? Especially when it sounds like it's your fault?" I shoot back, a spark of annoyance coming to life.

Luca runs his tongue over the front of his teeth and huffs. "I'm not blaming you. I'm pissed that you're hurt."

Oh.

His gruff answer should *not* make me feel… *fluttery*. Warm.

Slumping into the pillows at my back, I ask, "Why did Fabian do this when we're supposed to be married soon?" then take another sip of tea, praying for more calm.

"Because you're not marrying Fabian. You're marrying me. *I'm* going to be your husband. Not him."

CHAPTER TEN

LUCA

My timing could have been better.

Eden had just taken another drink of her tea when I dropped the news of our impending nuptials, causing her to spit it out and cough to clear her throat.

"What... did you... say?" she gasps, holding a hand to her mouth as her shoulders shake with the force of her coughing fit.

Placing a hand on her back, I rub circles over the smooth expanse in an attempt to soothe her nerves. "You will be my wife in seventeen days." That's the official date for the Marino-D'Amora wedding, even if it's a different D'Amora standing in as the groom.

"No, that's not right. The don—your father—told my dad that Fabian wanted to marry me. Not you."

"Fabian thought he could play games, but he lost. A match with me is far more profitable for our father, since it leaves Fabian open to a future arrangement that might provide a stronger alliance."

"I don't understand." Beanie nestled in Eden's lap, and immediately, she scooped the feline up to her chest, burying her face in the orange fur.

I knew it was the right decision to bring the cat to the manor. Once Dr. Bellamy assured me that Eden would be fine, I left my brothers to look after her while I fetched her cat. Beanie may be self-sufficient enough to survive a few days at home by herself, but I don't plan on letting Eden leave Blackchapel now that she's here.

The only reason I stayed away for so long was to keep her safe. A flimsy excuse that was shot to hell since she was hurt while I was pissing the time away at Delaney's.

That's not going to happen again.

Eden will remain safe and secure in the manor, where our security is top-notch, and I can personally keep an eye on her at all times.

Which necessitated a move for Beanie.

Packages of food, toys, and cat beds already littered my closet, hidden away from my brothers' prying eyes, in preparation for the day I could bring Eden to Blackchapel, so it was easy enough to transport the cat.

Plus, Allie already designated a room to her cat, Pretty Kitty. One full of scratch towers, elaborate shelving on the walls to sleep on, and dozens of toys. Beanie is still wary of Pretty Kitty, but she definitely enjoys the room.

Our timeline may have escalated, but I've been ready to have Eden by my side twenty-four-seven since the first moment I caught her reading at Enzo's birthday party. She'd been so beautiful sitting alone at a table hunched over her phone. I'd ambled behind her a couple of times to see what had captured her attention so thoroughly and found her deep in the middle of a book.

Beautiful and lonely.

Because even though her mind was occupied, an air of melancholy surrounded her in the midst of the party guests' revelry.

"My brothers and I run two organizations—Blackchapel Incorporated, which is a legitimate Fortune 500 company, and Blackthorn, an underground criminal organization. The don wants to call Blackthorn an ally, and a marriage between us solidifies the connection. Fabian will probably end up marrying some cartel princess or a Bratva daughter to cement those ties, instead."

Eden's brows lift dramatically above her amber eyes. "Brothers? Enzo has more illegitimate children?"

Of all the details she could latch on to, she chooses that one. Not the fact that I just admitted to being part of a criminal organization. But I guess that's to be expected from a woman raised within *The Family*.

"Not that I know of." A chuckle rumbles free. I hope I don't have any secret siblings running around the world. One asshole half-brother is enough. "These are brothers-in-arms. We're bonded by something deeper than blood—revenge against our bastard fathers. But you don't need to worry about that right now. All that matters is your healing."

I set the tray with tea and breakfast muffins on the nightstand as Eden readjusts on the bed. It's been an eventful twenty-four hours for her between her kidnapping and learning about our upcoming marriage, but my girl has taken it all in stride.

Because she's fucking amazing.

"I'd heal better in my own bed," she says hopefully, and while my intention is to give her anything her heart desires, I won't give her this. Eden is staying with me.

For good.

"Nice try, but you need to be monitored. The doctor said so."

"My mom can monitor me at home."

"Not gonna happen, Butterfly." Standing, I tuck the blankets around her, ignoring the stiffening of her muscles at my close proximity. "Get some rest. I'll be back in a few hours with lunch."

Eden stares skeptically at me, but I resist the urge to stay longer. She needs time to process.

"Do we know the names of the men who brought Eden to Delaney's?" I ask upon entering the den a few minutes later. It's a catch-all room with a huge television and fireplace on one wall, bay windows and bench seat on another, and a long wooden table that we use for planning a lot of our next steps.

"It's in your email." Rafe is our tech guy and is a pro at finding information, even if it means hacking into someone else's secured system. "They're low-level grunts, Tony Caparelli and Aldo Rossi. Tony and Fabian are gambling buddies. Bluewave Casino is their home away from home."

I scroll through the names, committing them to memory, then meet Jonah, Rafe, Mathias, and Hugo's serious gazes one by one.

"Who wants to join me on a scavenger hunt?"

***

We found Tony at Bluewave Casino just like Rafe suggested. Aldo was busy fucking a prostitute in a low-rent motel. Both men failed to put up much of a fight against five of the Blackchapel Bastards.

After combing through street camera footage from the night Eden was taken, we decided to recreate a few things for our unlucky hostages. Punches to the face and gut in a parking lot. Zip ties to the wrists. Tossed into the back of a van for transport.

Tony and Aldo probably thought they'd be dumped somewhere in D'Amora territory as a warning, but I'm not playing games with Fabian. This isn't a tit for tat. This is *You mess with my woman, death will follow*.

No mercy.

No excuses.

The trek through the woods surrounding Blackchapel Manor is chilly with the promise of winter right around the corner. Dead leaves crunch under our boots, attempting to overpower the garbled pleas from Tony and Aldo. My brothers and I have walked this path numerous times. First, as boys charged with following Conrad for one of his bloody lessons, and now as men who have accepted the crumbling chapel ahead as the home of our violent deeds.

Cracked stone litters the grounds, but we carefully navigate the labyrinth until we're at the front of the chapel near the altar. Hugo and Jonah toss Tony and Aldo onto the split steps and whip off the hoods covering their heads.

"Do you know why you're here?" I ask, withdrawing the blade from my belt. It's a simple pocket knife, not much to look at, but it gets the job done. I like that it's portable, no-nonsense. Just a good, old-fashioned tool always at my disposal.

Tony speaks first. "We're sorry about the girl, but come on, man. She's not worth all this." He raises his arms, his hands fisted tightly together against the bounds of the zip ties.

Mathias chuckles and relaxes on the front pew, prepared for the ensuing show. "He apologized then insulted your woman within the same breath. What an idiot."

"He works for Fabian. What do you expect?" An apathetic shrug lifts my shoulders. Squatting low, I address the two bound men. "Tell me, what did Fabian promise you in return for harming my girl? Money? Promotions within the organization?"

Aldo's gaze slices toward his buddy then back to me. "He paid off our gambling debts."

"Ah, you like hanging out at the Bluewave Casino, too? What was the amount? How much was Eden's sense of safety and perfect health worth?"

"A hundred grand," Tony mumbles.

"That's it?" My knife swings out to draw a thin line across each man's throat.

Not deep enough to kill them... yet.

They cry out in fear, the gravity of their situation finally sinking in. They won't be leaving this chapel alive.

Eden is priceless.

Worth more than one hundred grand. More than these two sniveling thugs.

She's mine to protect, and I already failed her once. I won't fail again. Starting with ridding the world of these lowlifes who dared to touch my woman.

CHAPTER ELEVEN

EDEN

Butterfly,
Rest and read. I'm told that these books are perfect for a day in bed.
I'll be home later this evening, but Allison will bring lunch to you at noon.
Yours,
Luca

The note was propped against a stack of books on the nightstand when I woke up. My name was scrawled across the front fold, though he'd switched to his random nickname for me inside the short letter. Flipping it closed, I set it aside and studied the colorful titles he left me. A mix of romantic comedies, fantasy romance, and some historical romance thrown in for good measure. *Someone else around here is a bookworm, too, apparently.*

"That was thoughtful of him," I say to Beanie who is sprawled out on the wooden dresser across the room. I don't even know how she got up that high. *Must have been one heck of a leap.* "But no matter how thoughtful he is, we're not falling for his charm. All the books in the world, catered meals, and—" I glance around the elegantly appointed room—"luxurious accommodations won't change our opinion of him if he doesn't release us."

A slow blink is the only response I get from Beanie.

Yeah, she doesn't care where she lays her head as long as her belly is full.

I am not so easily swayed.

My stomach growls as there's a knock on the door, and the smell of crispy bacon wafts in the air. Another protest of hunger from my belly.

Fine, I'll eat, but I won't be happy about it.

***

A FEW DAYS LATER

"Special delivery." Luca strides into the bedroom with a drink in one hand and a paper bag in the other. A familiar pink logo decorates the outsides of each, and an aggrieved sigh falls from my lips as I close the book I was reading by the window.

This room is enormous. Besides the massive bed, nightstands, and dresser, it also houses a cute little nook complete with two oversized, comfy chairs, a waist-high bookshelf, and a wooden coffee table. Honestly, the entire setup from the main sleeping area to the walk-in closet and bathroom suite could hold my entire one-bedroom apartment. All it's missing is a kitchen.

"You went to Baby Cakes?" I ask, already knowing the answer.

"You love their toasted marshmallow lattes and mini fruit tarts, so I figured I'd bring you a treat, since you won't be able to visit them for a while." He sets the drink and bag on the coffee table with a grin.

"Define *awhile*."

"Until you're healed and my wife." Luca settles into the chair next to mine, and his sapphire gaze leaves a trail of heat down my body as he catalogs my messy bun, borrowed plush robe, and ratty pajamas. Normally, I'd care more about my appearance, especially in front of someone as attractive as Luca, but my brain demanded I not give in to those urges.

Luca doesn't deserve to see me prettied up for his benefit, not when he's holding me captive.

"We're not getting married." The denial comes automatically. It's what I say every time he brings up our impending nuptials.

He's let me talk to my parents as long as I don't mention my kidnapping and subsequent stay at Blackchapel Manor, and they haven't said a word about me marrying Luca rather than Fabian.

Reaching forward for my drink, I wince at the pain in my ribs. Luca immediately notices and frowns. He grabs the cold coffee and lifts it to my lips.

I lightly swat his hand away. "I can manage by myself, thanks." The bruises leftover from my ordeal with Fabian's thugs are healing to an ugly yellowish color, but internally, it feels like I was punched just yesterday.

"You're hurt. Let me help you," Luca cajoles, shaking the icy drink. Reluctantly, I sip from the straw and swallow the sugary treat.

How did he even know this was my favorite flavor concoction?

***

MORE DAYS LATER

Credits start scrolling across the computer screen, and Luca sits up to press the spacebar to pause the video.

"Another episode?" he asks. Like it's another casual Tuesday night. Like we're a real couple watching TV in bed.

Covering a yawn, I shake my head. "I'm too tired, and this isn't a show you can just zone out of. There's too much you can miss."

Luca had recommended we binge-watch something my second night at the manor. After a ton of searching, we finally settled on a historical drama mini-series. The episodes were long and elaborate but definitely worth the time to untangle all the webs the characters wove.

Under different circumstances, I would have loved enjoying something so basic with Luca. He fit my idea of the perfect boyfriend, one who didn't mind my commentary during the show, and who even added his own wry observations.

But Luca isn't my boyfriend.

And nothing about this situation is normal.

The laptop snaps closed, and Luca rolls from the bed with a sigh. At first, I thought he might insist on sharing the bed with me, since this is his room judging by his clothes in the closet and shaving accoutrements in the bathroom. But he's never pushed for more. He leaves me alone each night like a gentleman.

It's unnerving—a jailer with a moral code.

Of course, maybe he just doesn't want to hear my squeaks of pain every time I toss and turn in the bed searching for a bruise-free, comfortable position to sleep in.

"Do you need anything before I go? Water?"

"No, I'm good. Thanks," I mutter, avoiding his careful perusal.

"Alright, if you change your mind, you have my number. Don't hesitate to text or call. I'm just across the hall." His fingers comb through his hair, ruffling the thick strands, then he steps forward to drop a kiss on the top of my head.

I freeze at the contact.

This is new.

"*Buonanotte, mia piccola farfalla. Prova a sognarmi, perché io sogno sempre te.*"

I'm still puzzling over what he said and processing the unexpected show of affection when he exits the room.

Nope, not normal at all.

CHAPTER TWELVE

EDEN

Fourteen days.

That's how long I stay cooped up in my gilded cage. A wounded bird—or *Butterfly* like Luca calls me—stuck in place. Not so much because the door barred me from escaping but because my bruised body couldn't work up enough willpower to leave the room. Even my short jaunts to the small sitting area knocks the wind out of me.

So, I hung out with Beanie, Luca when he brought meals or settled down to watch another episode of *Velvet Rose*, and occasionally Allison, who I learned also lived at the manor with one of the Blackchapel Bastards. My boss at the daycare reluctantly allowed me to use my PTO to cover the past weeks of absences, and the past two Sundays I called my parents like nothing was amiss. It implied an air of normalcy, except for the fact that I was stuck between two warring brothers, who also happened to helm dangerous criminal organizations.

"What do you think about running away?" I ask Beanie. She continues sunning herself beside the window with a plaintive meow. "Yeah, I didn't think so. You're firmly on Luca's side."

For some reason, my cat loves the man, despite being kidnapped from her very cozy and familiar home. We're two captives, although one of us clearly has succumbed to Stockholm Syndrome already.

But I refuse to submit to our captor, no matter how beautiful his dark eyes are or how sexy his perpetual shadow of a beard is. This Belle won't fall for the Beast—even if it's highly likely he's got a massive library hidden in this mansion, based on the number of books he's brought me.

What about when he's your husband?

"He's probably lying," I mutter to myself. No one's corroborated his story. Not that I've had much contact with the outside world to hear one way or another. But my parents haven't mentioned a change in grooms—only that wedding preparations are continuing without a hitch. After a recent phone call with my parents, where I once-again left out my current circumstances, it became obvious they were still under the assumption that I'd be marrying Fabian in three days, not his illegitimate half-brother.

Which leaves me questioning the truth of Luca's words.

Rolling to a sitting position on the side of the bed, I heave out a painful breath and clutch my side where a bruised rib has become the bane of my existence. This sharp twinge every time I move too much or breathe too deeply or freaking cough and sneeze is a *bitch*.

I allow myself a moment for the tenderness to ease then push to my feet with another gasp. I'm on a mission, and sore ribs aren't going to deter me—not anymore. My life is in confusing shambles at the moment, and it's not going to sort itself out while I lay in bed.

A wide hallway decorated with Baroque pieces greets me once I shuffle to the bedroom door. Glancing left then right, neither direction bears a clue of which way leads to freedom and fresh air. Hobbling to the right, it takes forever before a wooden balustrade appears accompanying a set of curved stairs.

This place is *peak* gothic romance.

It wouldn't surprise me to learn that ghosts haunt the halls or that Luca and his brothers are secretly vampires. Even my presence fits the narrative—the damsel in distress—though it'd be more romantic if a flimsy white nightgown dragged across the plush rugs rather than the worn hem of my sweatpants.

Snorting at my silliness, I descend the stairs, imagining myself a bit like Jane Austen's Catherine Moreland from *Northanger Abbey*—a young woman obsessed with gothic novels and the possibility of experiencing an extraordinary romance.

Too bad Luca doesn't have an ounce of Mr. Tilney in him.

Although I don't know Luca well, Mr. Tilney is a curate, a kind and funny man, whereas my captor is part of a group colloquially known as the Blackchapel Bastards. A name even I've heard of in my small corner of the world.

"Hey, you're up! How are you feeling?" Allie bustles into the grand foyer with several shopping bags in her hands before shutting the massive front door. I catch a glimpse of the intricate metal knocker in the middle of the dark wood, confirming my previous gothic appraisal of the home.

"Bored," I say, trying not to huff too loudly after the last step onto the marble floor. Those stairs are not a bruised rib's best friend. "Ready to go home."

Allie chuckles and nods in understanding. "Trust me, I understand exactly how you feel. When I first arrived at the manor, there were long stretches of playing video games with Rafe to stave off my brain melting from having nothing to do."

She'd shared a little of how she came to Blackchapel Manor and fell for the eldest Blackchapel Bastard, Mathias Beaumont during one of her visits to my room.

"We're surrounded by men with a penchant for kidnapping women," I quip.

"To be fair, Luca didn't seek you out like Mathias did me. You were thrown into his arms, and he decided to keep you." Her smile alludes to a belief that it was a perfectly logical thing for him to do.

Keep a woman.

Said woman definitely should not feel a twinge of warmth at being extraordinary enough to keep.

Gah, curse you, Catherine Moreland!

"I'm grateful for how he's helped me, but I'm much better now." My steps echo in the air as I follow Allie down the hall into a bright craft room surrounded by walls of ribbons, paper, and other creative supplies. It's the only modern space I've seen so far.

She drops her bags on an empty table and rolls her shoulders. "I know... But it doesn't make much sense to go home when you'll be his wife and move back into the manor three days from now, does it?"

"I'm highly suspicious there will even be a wedding. Don D'Amora hasn't said anything to me or my parents about a change in groom, and if everything stays the same, there's no way I'm marrying Fabian. Not after what he arranged to be done to me." A shudder wracks my body at the memory of his thugs' attack.

"I'm so sorry you had to endure that." Allie reaches out to squeeze my arm in comfort. "Know that Mathias and his brothers take revenge very seriously, especially when it comes to men who harm women."

"Luca mentioned something about revenge against their dads. What's that about?" I haven't thought much about that bit of information since he first explained his connection to Fabian and the don, but now it's relevant.

Luca has kept our conversations brief and light the past few weeks. Talking more about our nuptials like they're a done deal versus sharing what he does in between visits to me. In another life, I might find our chats comforting. Trust-building. But this is reality, and he's the man holding me here against my will.

"Do you want to sit and help me while we chat? I started crocheting these little stuffed animals to relax, then began donating them to the children at Polina's Place to give them a better home." Allie points to a framed photo on the wall of her and a group of smiling children proudly holding a zoo of animals ranging from elephants to tigers.

"That's amazing. Of course, I'll help. Just show me the pattern." My Nana taught me how to knit, crochet, and sew years ago as a little girl. There was even a lesson on creating the delicate lace Italy is known for. I never quite mastered the tedious process, but crocheting miniature animals for kids? I can definitely handle that.

Allie offers several patterns, and I choose the red panda—one of the cutest animals on the planet and a favorite of mine—before listening as she details the Blackchapel Bastards' background. How each man arrived at the manor as a boy. How they were forced to become ruthless mercenaries as kids. How it was all their fathers' fault.

"From what Mathias told me, it sounds like Luca had a decent childhood with his mom and dad before she died, then the don decided to pawn Luca off on Conrad rather than disrupt the life he had going with his wife and Fabian by bringing his eldest, but illegitimate, son home."

"I'm sorry to hear how Luca grew up, but he's still a stranger to me. Even these past few weeks, our conversations haven't lasted longer than the few minutes it takes for him to bring my meals and ensure I finish them. I don't truly know the man."

"But *he* knows *you*," Allie says, then flushes, ducking her head as if she didn't mean to blurt that out.

"What do you mean?"

She bites her lip and meets my curious gaze. "I probably shouldn't say anything, but since you're going to be married, I don't see how it would hurt... And you deserve to know... Did you receive some kind of fruit basket or bouquet recently?"

The question comes from so far out in left field that it's practically out of the stadium. "A fruit basket?" I laugh, pausing my stitches with the red yarn Allie gave me. "What does that have to do with Luca?"

"So, you did get one?"

My brows furrow. "Yeah, but from my apartment complex."

"Umm..." She draws the word out. "That wasn't from your apartment. The guys happened to see an order placed by Luca and put two and two together that he was interested in somebody."

"Okay, but that doesn't really make sense. Why would he send me a fruit bouquet, especially when my apartment complex has sent me all these other gifts, too?"

"Other gifts?"

Suddenly, I'm the one blushing. Like maybe I should have kept my mouth shut. "Yeah, there was a book for cat recipes and a butterfly suncatcher." As the words leave my mouth, they register with a different connotation in my mind.

A butterfly suncatcher.

Luca calls me *Butterfly*.

"No way." I shake my head in disbelief, but Allie keeps her mouth shut and hums in her throat in a knowing way. "No," I deny again. "Why would he send those things? It doesn't make sense."

"The guys think his little obsession started around the time his dad had his birthday party. Did you attend?"

"Of course, everybody in *The Family* did." *Including his bastard son*, I finish in my head the sentence that Allie is clearly holding back from saying.

The irony is if I hadn't been so engrossed in my mafia romance, then I might have heard the gossip happening in my own mafia family about Don D'Amora's illegitimate son appearing at the party.

I want to slap my forehead at how utterly clueless I've been. This is why I want separation from *Family* politics. I'm not cut out for this life of secrets and surprises.

Like the first gift showing up in my mailbox rather than with my leasing agent when she handed over a gift bag and folder welcoming me to the complex. Luca even impersonated a maintenance man to gain access to my home!

I've been so stupid.

"Luca has been sending me gifts since the Don's birthday party," I say flatly.

"And he might have been stalking you, too?" Her shoulders rise and fall in hesitation. "He's disappeared most nights. Everyone thought it had to do with a woman, so it's not much of a leap to assume he was going to see you."

"But I've never even met Luca before two weeks ago. He must have been going somewhere else." I leave out his maintenance visit, unwilling to share something that might confirm Allie's suspicions.

"Just because you didn't see him doesn't mean he didn't see you."

The words are quiet, but they roar in my head as my eyes widen at the implication. Luca stalked me. I have a stalker, and he's going to be my husband in three days. My fingers slip on the crochet hook.

"I've said too much." Allie grimaces and pats my shaking hand.

"No, thank you for telling me the truth." Because it's obvious Luca didn't plan to.

Like she read my mind, Allie adds, "I'm sure it would have come out eventually. Luca and his brothers aren't ones to keep their feelings a secret."

"Right," I say as I try to wrap my head around the fact that Luca has been watching me.

No wonder Beanie likes him. She must have seen him from a window and recognized him when Luca broke into the apartment to get her.

Oh my god. Was that even the first time Luca broke in? Suddenly, my too-real dream of somebody comforting me in my sleep doesn't seem so far-fetched.

My breathing becomes labored. My muscles tighten to the detriment of the poor red panda in my hands. How did my life come to this?

"This isn't what I want," I admit aloud. "My family is on the edges. I moved out of my parents' house to put distance between me and the mafia."

A sympathetic expression flashes across Allie's face. "And now you'll be tied even closer when you marry Luca."

"*If* I marry Luca."

"Unfortunately, I don't think you have much of a choice."

We'll see about that.

CHAPTER THIRTEEN

LUCA

Footsteps crunch the dead leaves that escaped the gardener's leaf blower. *It's like she wants to get caught*, I think, casually lounging against the corner of the manor.

Since Eden's arrival at Blackchapel, we've spoken almost every day, but for the past few, she's been suspiciously quiet, a panicky look growing in her eyes, and I know it's because of our wedding tomorrow.

Which is why I'm stationed outside tonight.

I've been waiting for my Butterfly to burst from her cocoon for weeks, and it looks like she's finally worked up the courage to try.

As if she could escape her future as my wife.

"Evening." I step out of the shadows in front of Eden. Beanie's cat carrier is held protectively against her chest.

"Luca," she squeaks. "What are you doing here?"

"Better question is what are you doing out here, bride of mine? You should be getting your beauty sleep before tomorrow's festivities."

Her throat works under the dim light of the moon. Eden opens her mouth then shuts it; she doesn't have a good reason for traipsing outside her room at one o'clock in the morning.

"Where did you plan on going?" I ask, curious to know the plan she's worked out. Her parents wouldn't harbor her for long. They're too loyal to the Don. Like everyone else in *The Family*.

Eden rocks on her heels before another round of courage straightens her shoulders. "It doesn't matter. We can't marry."

"You'd prefer my brother? The one who had his minions put their fucking hands on you then stuff you in the back of a van?"

"Of course not. I don't want to marry anybody. Not yet."

"Too bad, Butterfly. Your fate is sealed, and it's tied to mine."

"Please just let me go. Enzo will forget all about me, and you can finish your revenge against your dad and brother. I don't need to be involved."

"No." I step forward and pry Beanie out of her clenched hands, setting her on the ground beside us. Her pitiful mewling sounds throughout the night, but she's going to have to survive her enclosure for a little while longer.

Because our girl needs a reminder of who she belongs to.

CHAPTER FOURTEEN

EDEN

Pushing my escape to the last minute probably wasn't the smartest thing to do. But it took the past couple of days after my conversation with Allie to work up the nerve to try to slip free.

Unfortunately, I didn't slip far.

How did Luca know where I'd be?

He's your stalker. Of course, he knows where you are at all times.

The realization is at once terrifying and oddly comforting.

"You're not going anywhere except your bedroom," Luca says, crowding me backward until my back hits the rough brick of the manor. "Tomorrow, you'll become my wife, we'll leave for our honeymoon, and you won't attempt to leave me again. Understand?"

"Honeymoon?" Why is that the point that sticks out to me? Who cares about a romantic getaway when the getaway is with a man I'm being forced to marry? Who held me captive here for way longer than my injuries warranted?

"My father has graciously offered his villa in Torre delle Stelle for the next two weeks." The gleam of his white smile pierces the evening shadows.

Two weeks. Alone with Luca. In a foreign country.

Not happening.

I'm shaking my head before he's even finished his sentence. "I can't go to Italy. I can't marry you."

I can't. I can't. I can't.

Luca's heat penetrates the chill settling over my skin as he leans closer. The tip of his nose skims along my neck straight to my ear. "*Lo farai, bella ragazza. Non hai scelta.*"

My Italian is rusty, so the only word I understand is *bella*, but I doubt he said, *"You're right, beautiful. Let me take you home and forget all about this."*

"Luca..."

He groans, his hand on my hip tightening. *When did that get there?* "Say my name again, little Butterfly." His lips press beneath my jaw, and I shiver.

"Luca?" His name is a question this time because I don't know what the heck is happening. An hour ago, I made up my mind to escape Blackchapel, grab a rideshare home, then book it to a random hotel while I figured out what to do next. A life of vengeful siblings, murderous brothers, thoughtful stalkers, and arranged marriages would disappear into my rearview mirror as I fled Boston.

Except I've been caught, and a part of me is curious to know what a kiss from Luca would feel like. The love blind romantic that thrives on reading fictional stories of tough men obsessed with their women is throwing a freaking party in anticipation. Ugh, I can't succumb to his charms.

I can't. I can't. I can't.

Since when did I fall back into the same safe pattern my life followed before moving out of my parents' house? It's always been *I can't do this* or *I can't do that* because I'm a member of

The Family, I'm a girl, I'm too shy, I'm too boring. The list of excuses goes on and on, and I'm continuing the cycle.

I wanted a little adventure—not a dangerous, high-stakes one—but that's what I've got. And it comes with a sexy man who has only shown kindness so far, even if it's been peppered with overbearing bossiness.

Beanie's loud yowling continues in the background like she's begging me to finally see reason, so she can return to her cozy perch on the window seat in my room.

Another kiss.

This one tracing the edge of my mouth.

"Again," Luca commands, but he swallows my attempt to obey by capturing my lips with his. They're firm and warm and masterful in their possession as his tongue sweeps forward, teasing and tasting. "*Dolce farfalla*," he murmurs, retreating for a moment before stealing my breath again.

"Are we really getting married tomorrow?" I push against his broad shoulders to put an inch of distance between us. Not that it helps clear my head much. Luca's intoxicating scent wraps around me, the heavy bulge in his jeans presses between my thighs, and my lips tingle from his kisses.

"Yes, we are."

I nibble my bottom lip and Luca's gaze drops. Desire swells in the midnight centers. "I don't want Fabian there. I don't want to see him." *Ever, after what he orchestrated.* But I'm not sure how realistic that is when Luca's timeline for destroying his half-brother and Don D'Amora is unknown.

"Don't worry. He won't be in attendance. I talked Enzo into sending him on an errand after explaining how awkward his presence might be since there's been a switch in grooms."

"Oh." That was surprisingly considerate. But hasn't Luca been that way during my entire stay at Blackchapel? The opposing sides of him are a mystery—the stalker, the caretaker, the merciless killer intent on revenge.

And I'll have to learn how to live with all of them as his wife.

CHAPTER FIFTEEN

LUCA

"Sounds like your future mother-in-law is pissed." Mathias straightens my tie before patting my shoulder and stepping away. We're in a small room down the hall from the church altar, and Father Fado must have placed Eden's family right next door because her mom's shrill voice carries through the vents.

Mr. Marino's low murmur is harder to understand, but it's obvious he's trying to calm his wife.

Enzo must have shared the news with them. Instead of their daughter marrying the next D'Amora don, her husband-to-be is an illegitimate bastard.

"She'll get over it," I say, adjusting my cufflinks with the aid of the floor-length mirror attached to the wall.

"The mother is the least of his worries." Jonah takes a sip of the bourbon provided from a bar cart in the corner. I haven't attended many weddings, but I wonder if it's typical for a church to provide grooms and their entourage with liquid courage before exchanging vows. "His bride tried to escape last night."

Seated next to Jonah in a leather chair, Rafe's brows hit his hairline. "No shit? How far did she get?"

Mathias offers a tumbler of amber alcohol, and I nod in gratitude, glancing between the men who've become brothers to me. We're all here: Mathias, Jonah, Rafael, Hugo, and Dmitri. The only one missing is Aleksei. He's been undercover in prison for months, slowly working his way up the chain of command in Sergei Petrov—he and Dmitri's father's—illegal arms organization.

Unlike the rest of us, Aleksei's birth was kept a secret from Sergei. He's the only Blackchapel Bastard with that advantage. With the ability to secretly infiltrate his father's world.

"Barely five feet from the manor's perimeter. I figured she'd try to run, so I was waiting."

"Right... Forgot you're an expert at stalking the poor woman."

Everyone chuckles at Hugo's wry observation, until a knock on the door interrupts the moment of levity.

I check my watch. There's still twenty minutes before the ceremony officially begins. Does the priest want to go over the schedule again?

"Beaumont." My shoulders stiffen at the familiar voice once Mathias opens the door. "I'd like to speak to my son on his big day."

Mathias looks back at me with a silent question in his eyes. Let Enzo inside or bar his entry? Sighing, I gesture for him to let my dad in the room as the rest of the guys file out through a side door. Once we're alone, I lean casually against the back of a leather chair and wait for Enzo to speak.

"Your mother would have loved this. Her baby boy's wedding day."

"Don't mention *Mamma*," I warn, swallowing past the lump in my throat.

Enzo raises his hands in surrender. "I'm sorry, but I loved her, too, you know. That's why I kept these." He reaches into his jacket pocket, and I tense, for a moment wondering if this entire thing is a setup for him to shoot me dead in St. Michael's Parish. But instead of a gun, he removes a rectangular box and sets it on the coffee table between us.

"Go ahead. Open it." Enzo waits for me to cautiously grab the box and pop the top open. Inside are gold cufflinks with lion insignias. "Those belonged to your grandfather on your mother's side. They've been passed down in her family for generations, and she wanted you to have them for a momentous occasion. Your wedding day seems appropriate."

Tracing one of the tiny designs, a rush of emotion clogs my lungs. "You've kept these all this time?"

Enzo shrugs. "Like I said, I loved your mother." His face softens, and it's like the past few decades never happened. No abandonment at the manor. No murder lessons from Conrad. No drive for revenge against the man standing before me.

We're Luca and *Papà* again.

He's the hero I idolized.

A man I loved.

"Thank you," I mutter then hurry from the room without a backward glance, suffocating from memories I haven't thought about in years.

Forget about the past. Today is about the future.

Your future with Eden as your wife.

That's all that matters to me now.

CHAPTER SIXTEEN

DMITRI PETROV

Weddings aren't my thing. Women searching for their happily-ever-after. Men scoping out their next fuck. The only saving grace is the booze, and if there's one thing Enzo D'Amora has going for him, it's his excellent taste in liquor.

Sipping my brandy, I nod as the man continues extolling the benefits of the Boston Mafia joining with Blackthorn, the criminal organization I head with help from the rest of the Blackchapel Bastards.

"It's about time we band together, Petrov. I know there is bad blood between you boys and The Syndicate, especially after that messy business in Paris with Petit, but we're past that now." Enzo waves his hand magnanimously over the crowd of guests as if he didn't just brush over the death of one of his former friends and business partners during a firefight that also included my father, Sergei Petrov. Not to mention the assassination attempt on his eldest son. "Luca's thinking like a D'Amora now. With this marriage, we'll be unstoppable."

I don't correct his assumption, allowing a brief twitch of a grin to form.

Enzo and the rest of his associates will be ground into dust soon enough. Blackthorn doesn't form alliances. We don't play well with others. We fuck them over—especially those part of The Syndicate.

Spying Luca with his new bride, I abruptly excuse myself from the conversation and weave through drunken dancers across the dance floor. A few ladies duck their heads and avert their eyes as I pass.

A muscle pops in my jaw.

I'm used to being feared—the Blackchapel Bastards are notorious—but it's not just my reputation that scares women off. Some *like* the thrill of fucking a dangerous man. It's the fact that my face looks like it had a run-in with a meat tenderizer. Except the tenderizer was my bastard father's fists, before Mom got us out from under his thumb once she learned she was pregnant with my brother, Aleksei.

A brother currently locked up in prison while rising through the ranks of Sergei's illegal arms group. It's been over a year since I last saw my brother, though we manage covert phone calls every so often when he has an update for us.

Like when he rang to notify me about the added time to his sentence after getting in a fight. A brawl ordered by Sergei's inside man to test Aleksei's loyalty.

"Congrats to the newlyweds." I slap Luca on the shoulder and offer a smile to his bride.

"Thank you," Eden softly says as a pink blush stains her cheeks. Her traditional Italian lace wedding dress has sleeves and a high-neck that prevents anyone from seeing if the blush travels further. She's fully covered from the veil pushed back from her face to the tips of her white-slippered toes.

She's a beautiful bride, but the guests barely spared her a glance when she walked down the aisle with her father by her side. They were too intrigued by the switch in groom at the front of the church. Gossip ran rampant during the ceremony, and now at the reception.

"How does—Sorry, let me check this." My phone vibrates with a text message from Jessie over at Polina's Place, a safe house for women and children of domestic violence. Jessie manages the home while I'm a silent investor with Aleksei. Years ago, we both wanted to create something in honor of our mother, Polina, and a secure haven for abuse survivors—a place our family could have used—seemed like the perfect solution.

"Something wrong?" Luca asks.

"No, but I've got to go." Slipping my phone in my jacket pocket, I clasp his arm in farewell. "Enjoy Italy, you two." Then I exit the grand ballroom D'Amora secured for the reception, ignoring the trail of curiosity and horror that follows my footsteps.

CHAPTER SEVENTEEN

EDEN

After last night's wedding reception, Luca and I were driven to the airport by a Blackthorn soldier, where we boarded Blackchapel Inc.'s private jet for a nine-hour flight. Thankfully, Luca let me sleep alone in the bedroom while he handled final preparations for both of us taking the next two weeks off from work.

Yes, the *both* of us.

I'm not sure how he's going to smooth things over at the daycare when I've already used my PTO and sick days being cooped up at Blackchapel Manor. Maybe I don't want to know. Maybe he's blackmailing my boss into not firing me. I guess I'll find out when I eventually return to work.

Luca hasn't mentioned keeping me sequestered at the manor after our marriage, so I assume it's okay that I have a job.

Geez, more things I should probably discuss with my husband.

As if I don't already have a ton of questions.

"What's going to happen once you kill Enzo and Fabian? You'll run the mafia?" I ask before sipping the iced toasted marshmallow latte the flight attendant, Kurie, brought out, along with a breakfast of fruit and pastries. According to her, we'll land soon.

For my honeymoon.

Because I'm freaking married!

The giant diamond ring on my finger is still a shock. The ceremony and reception are a chaotic blip I've shoved behind me in favor of worrying about this trip. An international honeymoon where I'll be totally alone with my new husband.

My mom couldn't stop gushing about it in a vain attempt to seem calm after learning of the groom switch and flying off the handle. That had been an awkward and uncomfortable hour while donning my wedding gown at the church. My dad had maintained a wary but supportive facade once he'd eased Mom's concerns. Even if he disapproved of Luca, he'd never question the Don's decision.

Luca scoffs. "Hell, no."

A stricken expression courses over my features at his immediate denial. "You'll abandon all of those families? My parents? Not everyone is like your father or Fabian."

"They'll be offered the option of joining Blackthorn or continuing on with their lives without a crime organization pulling the strings. We'll provide a generous severance package," he says with humor, like it's a mere business acquisition versus the destruction of an entire way of life for people.

The Boston *Family* has been active for decades. They're a staple of the Italian-American community.

"I see..."

The pilot's voice crackles over the cabin's intercom system to let us know we're about to land, and I take the opportunity to look out the window. Bright azure blinks up at me with every gentle wave of the Mediterranean Sea. Rocky cliffs rise toward the sky. It's blindingly beautiful, and a tingle of excitement kindles at the bottom of my spine.

I've only been out of the country once. My high school English class took a trip to London during spring break to learn about William Shakespeare, Jane Austen, and dozens more British writers. It had been gray, rainy, and cold—the exact opposite of sunny Italy.

"Where exactly are we?" I ask, turning to meet Luca's intense gaze.

"Sardinia. Torre delle Stelle. We'll land at a private airstrip then have a thirty-minute drive to the villa. It's right on the beach, so I hope you packed a swimsuit." His eyes fall hungrily over my body, and instant heat flushes my cheeks.

Shrugging off the inconvenient attraction to my husband, I glance away, forcing myself to admire the gorgeous scenery below rather than Luca's handsome features. "You're better off asking Giulia. When I woke up yesterday, my suitcases were already packed."

Giulia is one of several maids who clean and cook for the manor, and we literally met two days ago, but I guess that's enough for her to pack for me—a total stranger. I'd peeked into the new luggage set, but at the sight of expensive silks and cozy cottons, an array of unfamiliar clothing, I'd zipped it right back up.

More evidence of Luca's stalking made my belly tumble, and the longer I looked at the new wardrobe that's most likely tailored perfectly to my size, the crazier the belly-tumbling got. My stupid romantic heart even tried to join in.

And that's the last thing I need to do... *Fall in love with my stalker husband.*

***

The click of the door opening then closing interrupts the peaceful lullaby of waves crashing along the shore below the bedroom balcony. I don't turn around to see who entered. There's only one person it could be.

Luca.

My husband must be eager to consummate our marriage after waiting a day and a half. We spent the afternoon exploring the villa and beach before an elaborate dinner was served to us on the luxurious patio overlooking the sea. Luca kept close with a hand on my lower back to guide me or a kiss to my temple every so often.

Each gentle caress heightened my awareness of him, and now I suppose it's time for the payoff.

A furnace of heat warms my back before two strong arms wrap around my waist. "Enjoying the view, *carissima*?" Luca's low murmur vibrates along my spine.

"I might as well soak it in while I can."

"Don't worry, we'll spend plenty of time exploring the island before returning home."

Home.

He means Blackchapel Manor. Not the apartment I was so proud of. The one I barely got to enjoy.

His hands skim over my belly to rest beneath my breasts, cupping the heavy weights in his large palms, and causing my breath to hitch in my chest. The memory of our kiss from the other night storms to the forefront to remind me how skilled this man is when it comes to my body.

He drowns me in sensations I've never felt before.

Addictive, too-good-to-be-real sensations.

"I can't wait to fuck these." Luca squeezes my breasts and pushes them together to form a deep valley and illustrate his crude meaning. "Your tits will look so pretty covered in my cum, Butterfly. Reddened from the rough slide of my cock then extra creamy from my seed."

This man is *dirty*.

Filthy.

Sexy.

No one has ever spoken to me like this, and frankly, I doubted anyone ever would. I'm not the type of woman to elicit raging passion or even a moderate interest. Men ignore wallflowers like me.

At least they did.

Until Luca.

One hand continues to massage my breast, a thumb circling my nipple before flicking the tip, as another hand slides lower to dip between my thighs. Giulia packed an assortment of outfits I'd never seen before, including silky nightgowns like the lavender one a soft breeze from outdoors is currently molding to my curves. The flimsy fabric immediately clings to my wet folds with the firm, possessive clasp Luca takes of my pussy.

"Mmm... Already soaking wet for your husband?" His lips rasp over my neck to my ear, his beard scratching the sensitive skin. "Such a good girl, my sweet little wife."

"Luca..." I'm not sure what I want to say. Don't stop? We shouldn't do this? My conflicting emotions threaten to give me a headache when all I really wish for is relief from the stress of the past few weeks. After all, what's done is done. Whatever my fears going into this marriage, they didn't put a stop to it.

For better or worse, I'm married to Luca—my stalker, my protector.

Do I really want to keep fighting him and my attraction?

A resounding *no* echoes in my head. I hate conflict. I've avoided it for most of my life. Truthfully, I've been a bit of a pushover except for these last few months when I stood up to my parents and moved out on my own.

I don't want to be a doormat for my husband, which is why I've railed against our union and chosen to ignore the kind things he's done for me—not the least of which was caring for my injuries after Fabian's ordered beating.

"Stop thinking, Eden." There's a sharp nip to my earlobe, and I jerk to attention. He's right. Thinking has gotten me nowhere with him. With this whole situation.

So, I might as well give in, right? Accept the path my life has taken and revel in the pleasure of Luca's desire. Because what other choice do I have?

"Make me," I dare, desperate to forget about right or wrong and just feel for once in my life.

Luca growls, then I'm snatched into the air and tossed on the bed like a tiny ballerina flying across stage rather than the lumbering baby elephant I sometimes feel like. He strips off his shirt but leaves his pants unbuttoned to hint at the bulging arousal his happy trail leads to.

"You just waved a red flag in front of a raging bull, Butterfly. Let's pray you don't regret it." One minute, Luca is standing beside the bed, outlined by a glow of moonlight, and the next, his shadowed face hovers over mine while his heavy body presses me deeper into the mattress.

The thin straps of my gown snap under his strength, cool air rushing over my flushed chest, before Luca's hot mouth captures a pebbled nipple and laves it with his tongue.

"Oh, god!" I arch into him, staring up at the sheer curtains draped over the four-poster bed. My hands clench around his broad shoulders as they bunch and shift with each move of his head between my breasts.

"So rosy and sweet," he murmurs, alternating between leisurely licks and powerful suction until I feel raw and over-sensitized and desperate for release.

"Luca... Stop teasing..."

"But it's so much fun." His dark chuckle wafts across my abdomen once he finally begins a trek lower. Instinctively, my legs widen to welcome him where I need him most, and I don't care how wanton it makes me.

I'm a virgin who is now married to the hottest man I've ever met. A man obsessed with me, based on Allison's comments and Luca's own behavior. So, sue me if I'm ready to be *fucked* into oblivion on my Italian honeymoon.

"There she is." Luca's breath settles over my pussy, a whisper through the crop of curls there. "My brave Butterfly opening up for me," he groans and nuzzles a cheek into the crease of my thigh. "I've dreamt of this moment. Jerked off to the thought of eating your hot little cunt until you screamed my name. And now you're going to give me what I want, aren't you, sweet Eden?"

"Y-Yes..." I stutter, wound too tightly to speak coherent sentences.

"Good girl." He spreads me wider until the sound of my drenched pussy reaches my ears, and I moan at the obscenity.

The wet tip of a tongue edges around my clit before wedging beneath the tingling bundle of nerves to start an insistent pattern meant to make me whimper from pleasure overload.

L. U. C. A.

Is he spelling his name?

Two fingers tease the walls of my pussy, searching for that one special spot, and when Luca finds it, I almost buck him off the bed from the onslaught of sensation.

"That's right, *carissima*. Fuck my face. Ride my fingers. You can bend and wiggle all you want, but I'm strong enough to withstand it."

"Stop... talking," I order, shoving his head back between my legs. I might worry about being too aggressive, except Luca releases another primal rumble from his chest and intensifies his efforts to get me off.

Adding a third finger to stretch my tight muscles.

Sucking my clit like it's a damn popsicle.

He keeps me on the edge of bliss until I can't stand the pressure anymore and every cell ignites in flame. Rather than dragging the orgasm out with his sinful mouth, Luca rises enough to free his cock from its restraints, notching it to my still-spasming channel.

Maybe I should've told him I'm a virgin.

Maybe he would've been gentler.

But then his thick cock buries deep in one powerful thrust, and *should've, would've, could'ves* are the furthest things from my mind.

There's a slight burn from stretching around his wide girth, but it's not as bad as I feared. Guess the few times I worked up the courage to use my neon pink dildo paid off because the edge of pain is bearable compared to the first time I ever stuffed something in there.

"Goddamn, you're tight," Luca huffs, his muscles straining to maintain a semblance of control. A drop of sweat gleams on his temple under the pale lighting, and my walls clench reflexively at the notion of licking it away. Of licking every part of my husband's chiseled body.

"Fuck, do that again."

I comply and enjoy the wash of pleasure-pain on his sharp features. I hold power over this man—a realization that I'm only now beginning to understand.

"Move, Luca. I need—"

"What do you need? Tell me." The way he immediately cuts me off should be annoying, but it's obvious how obsessed he is with pleasing me that I can't even fault him for needing to know the answer *now*. Not able to wait the few seconds necessary for me to complete a sentence.

"I need you to fuck me," I say, a blush blooming on my cheeks at what I'm about to voice. I'm not a demonstrative or vocal person, but Luca's unfiltered promises and fantasies encourage me to be just as brazen. "Fuck me so hard that my pussy threatens to go on strike tomorrow because it's so sore. Do you know that kind of fucking?"

"Be careful what you wish for, baby." Luca's hand anchors around my neck and gently squeezes. My breath hitches in my lungs. The vulnerable position doesn't scare me; it only makes me hotter.

Rising slightly to increase the pressure of his hold, I lick my lips and swallow, shivering at the warm press of his palm along the fragile arc.

This is it.

I'm going all in.

Luca thrusts harder. Faster. Until the bed rocks against the wall, a banging melody that overpowers the ocean waves outside.

"Come for me, baby. Come for your husband."

With another cry, my body tenses, then bright relief floods my veins, the tension breaking as Luca jerks and curses, following with his own orgasm.

Jets of cum slicken my thighs to mix with my arousal. It's sticky and warm, and I feel deliciously dirty.

Deliciously *claimed*.

My stalker husband's prized possession.

CHAPTER EIGHTEEN

LUCA

"So... Allie told me some things..." Eden's hesitant voice fades in the quiet room. Our breathing has finally slowed to a normal pace after the frenzy of our lovemaking, and her head rests on my chest, her soft waves tickling my skin.

I've dreamed of moments like this for so long that I can hardly believe it's real. Eden is mine. My wife.

"What things exactly?"

"Like you... stalking me?"

A burst of chagrined laughter puffs out. "Damn Mathias and the rest of them." Their meddling is the reason my personal business has been bandied about the manor like we're in fucking middle school.

"So, it's true," she says flatly, and I half expected her to roll away from me in fear. It's one thing to be forced into marriage after I kept her secured at Blackchapel; it's another to add *stalker* to the list of *warden* and *husband*.

"If it makes you feel any better, I don't make a habit of stalking women." I scrub a hand over the scruff on my face. I haven't trimmed since yesterday, but Eden didn't seem to mind the unruly scrape on her inner thighs as I ate her out, and frankly, my marks on her body makes me a bit feral.

My cock hardens in agreement, but now's not the time for round two.

Eden wants answers, and I'll do anything to ease her concerns.

"You caught my attention at Enzo's birthday party," I start. "A beautiful woman reading on the fringes of a crowded room. You never noticed how often I circled around you, trying to keep you in view amidst Enzo and his friends' interference. What was so intriguing about that book, Butterfly?"

"*The Mafioso's Heart*," she says in a sheepish voice. "Sometimes I like reading about *happily ever afters* in the mob since reality is so different."

"It doesn't have to be." *Happily ever after* is exactly what I want for us.

"Perhaps..." Her finger traces my pec then pokes it. "What happened after the party?"

"It didn't take much to figure out who you were, where you lived. The trees surrounding your home provided ample cover for—" I cover a cough of embarrassment. Admitting to spying on Eden is uncomfortable as fuck.

"Invading my privacy? Did you ever enter my apartment? Is that why Beanie likes you so much?"

"She has good taste? I only broke in once, but it was to check on you. Your patio door was left unlocked," I say as if that's a good excuse for breaking into her home while she slept.

"Why were you checking on me?"

"You cried for three days straight. I'm guessing this was after you found out about the arranged marriage to Fabian." The mention of my half-brother puts my teeth on edge. He has no place in our marriage bed.

"Yeah, it was. I thought I dreamed somebody had been in my room, but you were actually there. And the gifts?"

"Guilty," I admit.

"What about fixing my dishwasher? How did you know about that?"

"I installed monitoring software on your computer months ago. So, when your request came through, I hacked into the property management company's maintenance system. I didn't want strange men hanging out in your apartment while you were alone."

"Versus one man watching my every move. God... I've been so clueless. It's a miracle I've only been kidnapped once in my life since I never noticed having a freaking stalker."

"Don't beat yourself up. I took great lengths to stay hidden. And you shouldn't have been kidnapped even once. That's on me not protecting you better." I'd considered placing a tracker on her phone along with cameras around the apartment complex, but the war between allowing Eden a semblance of privacy and my overbearing protectiveness stopped me from doing so.

And my girl paid for it.

Eden sighs. "Is there anything else I should know about? Speak now, then we can move forward with no more secrets..."

"That's all, I promise. Unless you want to know more about the plans to dismantle the Boston Mafia *Family* along with their ally, The Syndicate. Allie only ever wants to know the basics, but if you'd like details..."

"No, I'm good for now, but thank you." She covers a yawn. Her lashes flutter closed. "And thanks for the gifts, even if their delivery was questionable. You didn't have to do that."

I stroke her hair as she falls asleep in my arms.

Eden's wrong.

I did have to send those gifts. Because she's my girl, and every instinct inside me says to spoil her. To protect her. To provide for her every need.

Those few presents were only the beginning, a fraction of what my wife deserves.

***

DAYS LATER

"Why do you watch these?" My palm rests on Eden's stomach, the warmth of my hand helpful for her cramps. It sucks that her period started on our honeymoon, but it'll take a lot more than some blood to stop me from fucking my wife every chance I get.

Something she'll learn soon enough.

"ASMR videos help me relax. They're soothing."

"Lounging on the beach isn't relaxing enough for you?" The villa boasts a private beach where we've spent several hours this afternoon on a massive canopied bed. House staff set up a small table full of fruit, cheese, wine, and water, and I've been vigilant with ensuring Eden's pale skin is properly covered in sunscreen. "It all works in tandem."

I'll take her word for it as I leave Eden to her videos and focus on rubbing soothing circles over her lower abdomen.

"Why did you skip that one?" I ask several minutes later.

The previous video had two young women in low cut tanks. One girl began massaging the other's shoulders and chest. It verged right on the line of inappropriate for a public forum, though based on the number of likes I saw before Eden swiped up, viewers didn't mind.

"Videos like that one make me uncomfortable. The women are overly exposed unlike the usual clips, and there's almost this dead look in their eyes." Eden shrugs a shoulder. "Maybe I'm reading too much into a sixty-second shot, but I'd rather watch something that gives me positive tingles rather than negative vibes."

"Positive tingles?"

"That's what all the ASMR people call it. Tingles. I liken it to goosebumps from feeling good."

We watch a few more videos when Eden shifts with a quiet groan. Her phone falls to the bed as she rolls to her back and scrunches her eyes closed.

"Cramps still being a bitch?" My hand adds a little more pressure to her stomach like I can physically stop her pain.

"Yeah. I wish the ibuprofen would kick in already." She'd popped a few pills about a half hour ago when the pain ratcheted higher.

"Would a different kind of distraction help?"

"Like what?"

"Like orgasms."

"I'm on my period, Luca."

"I know. That's why we're having this conversation."

She shades her eyes as she looks up at the clear sky, her brow wrinkling in confusion. "We're outside."

Oh, my innocent little Butterfly.

CHAPTER NINETEEN

EDEN

The Mediterranean Sea sparkles under the midday sun, but its warmth combined with my period hormones add a sweaty film to my skin that doesn't lend itself toward feeling sexy. That doesn't seem to bother Luca, though, as one of his hands abandons my cramping stomach to wedge between my legs.

"We could be in the middle of the Colosseum with an audience of thousands, and I'd still want to fuck you," he murmurs, his teeth scraping across the fluttering pulse in my neck. "I don't care where we are. If you're on your period or not. I crave every part of you, and nothing will stop me from claiming it."

My thighs clench as a gush of arousal and blood seeps out. Period cup be damned in the middle of my husband's seduction, apparently. The ache in my lower abdomen pulsates in time with the throb of my clit.

Luca's proposition is scandalous yet tempting.

I've used orgasms in the past to alleviate period pain—the rush of endorphins, a welcome respite—but obviously that was in the safety of my room, locked behind a closed door, and alone in my bed.

What Luca's suggesting...

My sensitive nipples brush against the spandex of my bikini—two scraps of fabric I never would have chosen for myself, but all the bathing suits Giulia packed were laughably tiny. Something else Luca didn't seem to mind.

"Open for me, *carissima*. Let me take care of you." The hot breath of his command washes over my ear as his broad palm contracts around my pussy, grinding into my clit.

"Not here," I pant with a lick of my dry lips. The white canopy drapes dance on a light breeze, and I latch on to the cooling temptation of the sea crashing against the sandy shore. "In the water."

No one but us occupies this stretch of beach, but at least, I'll have an illusion of privacy underwater. Maybe it'll help me cool off, too.

Luca pauses and glances between me and the clear blue water. "Fine." Carefully, he disentangles himself from my body to stand and strip away his swim trunks. Naked. Proud. He motions to my bikini. "Your turn."

My husband is a Roman god.

Glistening golden skin armors his body. Defined pectorals, ridged abdomen leading straight to the steel root of his cock. Slabs of thick muscles bunch around his shoulders and taper into the strong arms that have effortlessly carried me around Blackchapel Manor or tossed me on the master bed inside the villa.

Luca is a gladiator of old, and he's waiting for me to bare myself to him as if I were a prize to be won. A goddess to match his divine nature. Except I'm fluffy, not toned. And currently bloated like a balloon.

"Actually…" I start to backtrack. This isn't a good idea.

"If you're about to change your mind, stop. There's only one choice here: take off that bikini or I shred it to pieces. Either way, you end up in the water with my cock filling that sweet little pussy of yours."

God, why does every word out of his mouth have to be so damn sexy?

I can't think straight when he's all growly and dominant and determined to get what he wants. Especially when what he wants is to pleasure me.

Rolling to my knees on the soft daybed, I watch Luca's gaze darken and cling hungrily to my neck, where my fingers fumble with the tie of my top. The flimsy strings quickly separate, but I catch them before letting the two triangle pieces fall and exposing my chest to Luca, the sun, and the seagulls squawking in the sky.

"Be brave, Butterfly." The gentle encouragement eases my nerves, and I release the floral-printed ties. A string of Italian spouts from Luca. "*Cristo, presto scoperò quelle tette grosse.*"

Do I have any clue what he just said? Nope.

Does it still make me horny as hell? God, yes.

"What does that mean?"

A devilish grin appears on his tan face. "We need to work on your Italian, Butterfly. I said, '*Christ, soon I'm going to fuck those fat tits.*'"

"Oh. Um..." How do I respond to that? *Yes, please?* "You're quite fascinated with my breasts."

"I'm *quite fascinated* with every luscious inch of you." Luca stalks closer, making me wonder if he thinks I'm stalling and he's about to fulfill his threat of shredding what's left of my bikini, but instead of reaching for the ties at my hips, he braces his fists on the bed on either side of my spread knees and sucks a nipple into his greedy mouth.

"Luca!" My fingers dive into his ruffled hair as my head tips back on a moan. What a picture we must present—me on my knees with my back arched, breasts crushed to Luca's bearded face while his teeth and lips nip and soothe.

A husband—*my husband*—marking his wife. Painting my pale flesh with little red love bites. Each one a direct line to my clit until the dozens of threads form a knot of desire that tightens with each pull of his mouth.

My pussy contracts, closing around nothing except my period cup. Unfulfilled. Aching.

"We're not going to make it to the sea, little Butterfly. My garden of paradise is right here with you," Luca growls, flipping us around so I face the water while he climbs behind me. The snap of spandex digs into my love handles before my bikini bottoms disappear.

Guess he made good on his promise, after all.

"Bend over, *carissima*, and spread those thighs nice and wide." His heavy hand guides me down until my swaying breasts graze the bedsheets in a tantalizing tease. "Watch the waves. Imagine floating in their cool depths." He gently rocks me back and forth to mimic the rhythmic tides, lulling me into a relaxed dream state.

Until the wet heat of his tongue glides through my folds to lap from my sex all the way to the shadowy cleft of my ass. I jump at the unexpected sensation.

He put his mouth *there*.

He licked my—

"Mmm... Copper and honey." Luca kisses up my spine then bites my earlobe. "Remember this, *la mia piccola farfalla*, you belong to me. Your beautiful body is mine. I'm going to lick, suck, and fuck every one of your holes, and you're going to love it. Crave it. Become addicted to me like I am to you. Understand?"

"Y-Yes, Luca," I stutter, stunned by the feral need in his voice.

"Yes, *husband*," he corrects, and I shudder at how possessive he sounds.

"Yes, husband." The words are barely spoken before Luca removes my period cup and replaces it with his thick length stretching my pussy wide for his invasion. The rubber device is tossed to the sand, my blood spilling in a barbaric scene of scarlet to stain the pristine beach.

My fingers dig into the bed for purchase and hang on as he takes his cues from the sea and pummels deep inside like a hurricane battering the shore.

"I will never tire of hearing you call me your husband, *wife*." He grunts and growls, our flesh slapping together, sloppy, wet heat dripping down my thighs.

Arousal, blood, and soon, Luca's seed.

CHAPTER TWENTY

LUCA

My wife's juicy ass bounces with each harsh thrust of my hips, and the sight of my cock glistening pink with her arousal and blood has an animalistic roar bellowing from my chest.

Reaching beneath her soft belly, I search between damp curls to find her clit and circle the sensitive bud. Eden whimpers and sinks lower on the bed until her cheek rests on the mattress, her labored breathing rustling the strands of hair tangled around her head in a halo.

"Come for me, little Butterfly. Come for your husband."

Eden tenses then cries out as another rush of wetness soaks my cock. Her body shakes beneath mine. Trembling curves. Flushed skin. My girl is gorgeous in her pleasure, and she's all mine.

When the tight clamp of her cunt triggers my own release, I shout in satisfaction and come deep inside her pussy, pulling out at the last second to cover her ass and back with the final blasts of my cum.

"Luca..."

"I'm here, *carissima*," I murmur, rubbing the warm mark of my ownership into her pretty skin before collapsing on my side to meet her drowsy eyes. "How are you doing? Are you okay? I wasn't too rough, was I?" I wanted to erase the pain of her period, not add to it.

"You were perfect." She hums low in her throat. "Though I might live on this beach now. I can't move."

Chuckling, I gently unfold her tired limbs then hoist her higher into my arms.

"What are you doing?" Her disgruntled grumbling is adorable as I tread through the sand until we hit the turquoise water.

"We're cooling off in the Med. Just relax, I've got you."

Her eyes close in an act of trust as her body softens in my grip. I'll never take Eden's trust lightly.

Her legs hook around my waist as she drops backward to float on the gentle waves. My hands caress her generous love handles as I admire the beautiful sight of my wife, relaxed and satisfied. Rock formations jut into the water on our left while green hilltops rise toward the clear blue sky. I have to give Enzo credit; he sure knew how to pick the perfect Italian getaway spot.

Everywhere I look is a picture-perfect scene, though the best view is right in front of me.

A particularly aggressive wave hits my back, and we stumble forward. Instinctively, Eden's grip tightens.

"Don't let me go."

"Never, baby." My hands tenderly squeeze her hips to prove my point. "I will always keep you safe."

Until my dying breath.

CHAPTER TWENTY-ONE

EDEN

The bare back of a woman appears on the screen, and my eyes feel heavier as I watch the rhythmic motions of a massage therapist working on their patient.

Soft candlelight flickers across them to create a cocoon of serenity. The dim lighting isn't as harsh on my eyes as some of the bright fluorescents other creators use in their videos, and it all works together to make me sleepier.

Luca likes to tease me about these ASMR videos, especially since I don't even have the volume turned up to listen, but it's not the sound that soothes. It's the repetitive movements.

"Watching on mute again?" Luca murmurs from behind me. His arm is a muscled bracket around my stomach as he nuzzles into the crook between my neck and shoulder. I'm still getting used to sleeping with someone else in my bed, but it's not an unpleasant sensation. My husband is warm and snuggles around me like a weighted blanket.

Pressing a finger to the button on the side of my phone, sound plays on the next video. "Happy now?" Typical spa music fills the air—chimes mixed with low bass notes—as a young woman wearing a cropped tank rubs another woman's shoulders. Her arms rest on the massage chair, and a glimmer of green on her wrist catches my eye.

Luca feels me stiffen and asks, "What's wrong?"

"I... I don't know." A hazy memory wisps to life in elusive threads I try to follow back in time. My kidnapping. The smell of eucalyptus. Someone wearing a jade bracelet with a Q charm.

Just like the girl in this video.

I sit up with a gasp and throw my phone on the comforter as if it burned me.

"That bracelet. I recognize it, or something similar." Suddenly, the discomfiting feelings I've had watching previous videos form a jagged puzzle. Like my subconscious has been warning me of something all this time. "It triggered a memory from my kidnapping. There was another victim in the van with me, and she wore the exact same bracelet that woman is wearing. I'm not the only woman Fabian's ever held hostage. I think... This is going to sound crazy, but I think he might be forcing women to make videos."

"For ASMR?" Doubt tinges the edges of Luca's tone.

"I'm not sure. I just... Never mind." I force myself to lay back down and face the wall. I sound ridiculous. First, I forgot about that poor girl in the van with me, and now I think I'm seeing her in a random internet video. Assuming she's in trouble because the entire spa setup gives me bad vibes.

Clearly, I need to lay off the true crime docs if my paranoia leads me to imagining sketchy things from a thirty-second massage clip.

"No, don't shut me out." Luca uses his hand on my belly to roll me over. His concerned face hovers over mine in the pale moonlight. "It wouldn't surprise me to learn that Fabian is involved in trafficking or a prostitution ring. Criminals use innocuous things all the time as cover for their illegal dealings.

We just have to figure out how, or if, these videos fit into things. I'll have one of the guys check it out."

My brows wing into my hairline. "Really? It's a longshot that any of this means something. It's probably a coincidence that this woman has the same bracelet. And just because I got a bad feeling doesn't mean—"

A rough-tipped finger lands on my lips. "Stop. Stop doubting yourself. We'll check it out. Even if the only thing to come of it will be your peace of mind."

"Thank you," I whisper, confused and flattered by his vote of confidence.

Luca drops a kiss to my temple then returns to his previous position of cuddling close to my side. "You don't need to thank me. I trust your instincts, and there's not much I won't do to ensure your happiness and safety. Looking into a couple of ASMR videos is nothing."

It's not nothing to me.

If I brought such a flimsy concern to my family, they'd brush it off as a silly bout of paranoia. My parents love me, but they also consider me sheltered and naive, which to be fair, isn't far off, since they're the ones who kept me close to home. They don't see me as a competent adult. I'll always be their quiet little girl.

But Luca sees me.

He *trusts* me.

It's a frightening and exhilarating realization.

CHAPTER TWENTY-TWO

JONAH ANDERSON

"Are you ready for this?" I ask Hugo. He agreed to accompany me on this recon trip to the warehouse Rafe found deep in Fabian's books. The building sits on the edge of the city, buried between a dozen other structures and shipping containers. Salt and oil mix in the air as the clanking of metal-on-metal echoes from the moored ships further down the waterline.

Hugo gives a small nod, never one to waste a breath on sentences if it can be helped, and we creep forward.

Fabian's security is shit—two men relaxing in front of the metal entrance. Surely, if Luca's half-brother kept anything of importance here, like trafficked women, he'd invest in better protection, right?

Swift shots to the forehead and heart down each man with a thump to the ground. Hugo and I step over the corpses to test the door. Unlocked.

"What the fuck?" I mutter under my breath. This feels too easy, which has my hackles rising. Nothing in our world runs this smoothly.

A quick search of the building reveals it's empty, which explains the lack of security detail, but the three rooms decked out like a spa retreat makes me think Eden's hunch about women being forced to film is right.

"What is all this?" Hugo asks, picking up a bottle of eucalyptus oil, sniffing it, then setting it down with a wrinkle of his nose.

"Not sure yet. Let's check out the back by the docks."

As soon as we're outside again, the sound of voices cracks the air, becoming louder the closer we get. So, this is where all of Fabian's men are—guarding two shipping containers that I can only imagine has the missing women.

"Fuck," Hugo breathes.

"My sentiments exactly." Reaching into my pocket, I text Dmitri that we need backup from Blackthorn. Hugo and I are good, *deadly*, but there's no way we can take out a contingent of men and rescue whoever's in those containers. Luca is next on my list to notify of this new development.

Despite being happily ensconced in his newlywed bubble, he'll want to know about this. He'll want a chance to disrupt his half-brother's disgusting operation, even if he and Eden only landed back in Boston mere hours ago from their honeymoon trip to Italy.

My phone lights up with a message, but instead of Dmitri's or Luca's confirmation, it's a text from Valerie—the curvy journalist intent on exposing my politician father for the fraud he is.

She's also the woman you shouldn't have kissed.

I've been blaming high emotions after she was almost killed during a meeting with me, Mathias, and Allie, but the excuse is flimsy at best. Emotions have never clouded my judgment before, even in ambush situations like what happened at that cafe with Valerie.

VALERIE: *The article will go to print in a month. My editor wants to wait until we're closer to the election date to really screw with your dad. Can't say I'm excited to wait, though.*

ME: *Join the club, tiger, but patience is key. He'll get what's coming to him.*

VALERIE: *So bloodthirsty. LOL*

My little tiger has no idea...

CHAPTER TWENTY-THREE

LUCA

That evil bastard.

Fabian is fucked in the head, so the fact that he's involved in the flesh trade isn't a total surprise. You'd think after a childhood of violent lessons where Conrad taught us how to murder and manipulate men that nothing would shock me anymore.

But the sight of these shipping containers being filled with women is hard to watch.

And, to think, Eden accidently discovered this entire operation based on weird videos on the internet and a victim's bracelet.

When Jonah texted me, I'd slipped from our bed to dress and drive to the docks for the takedown. The flight from Italy to Massachusetts had been long, and Eden fell asleep almost immediately upon our arrival at the manor—Beanie snuggled close to her chest.

Never one to be far from my wife, I'd joined them for a nap until Jonah's late-night message.

"Nathaniel and his team are in position. Everyone ready?"

Dmitri took point the moment he arrived at the docks with Blackthorn reinforcements. Affirmatives ring out over the comm line, and anticipation buzzes through my veins, a live wire prepared to burst free and wreak havoc.

Tonight will be another dose of payback to Fabian for what he did to Eden, since I already dealt with the thugs who hurt her. It'll also serve as a foreshadowing of what's to come for the entire D'Amora organization, then The Syndicate.

Take no prisoners. Total decimation.

Dmitri gives the signal. He and I flank one container while Jonah and Hugo move to another. The D'Amora guards aren't expecting trouble based on the lazy way they lounge around the dock. I wonder how many shipments have passed through here without a hitch for them to be so comfortable.

The likelihood of dozens of victims causes bile to rise in my throat, but I swallow it down, focusing on what I can control—saving these women tonight—versus what might have happened in the past.

Sneaking up behind a man lighting a cigarette, my knife slices across his carotid artery in a whisper-soft swish. A gurgle of blood follows before he drops to the ground. Like a game of dominos, each unlucky D'Amora bastard tumbles until only Blackthorn men remain in a field of bloody bodies.

We usually send a clean-up crew to wipe away the evidence of our presence, but not this time.

We want Fabian to see the carnage.

We want everyone to know that the Blackchapel Bastards won't stand for human trafficking in our city.

***

It's dawn by the time I return to the manor. Dmitri and the rest of the guys are transporting the women we found to Polina's Place—Dmitri and Aleksei's safe haven for victims of abuse—but they don't need my help anymore. I've got my own woman to check on. Especially after witnessing the terror cloaking those we rescued.

The bedroom door silently opens to reveal Eden sprawled across our bed with Beanie holding court at the bottom of the mattress, her intelligent eyes tracking my steps. She must have had enough of Eden's cuddling and decided to keep watch as her mistress's sentry.

"It's been a while since you've caught me sneaking into our girl's room, huh?" I whisper, petting her soft head. She's used to my clandestine antics. Beanie purrs, butting herself harder into my scratches, while I let the night's activities drift away, enjoying the immediate peace just being near Eden causes.

Pale yellow light creeps over the floor and comforter in a single beam to highlight Eden's relaxed features. Her mouth is slightly open, slow and steady puffs of air filling the quiet. Her fingers hold a fistful of the charcoal blanket under her chin.

She looks so innocent. *Angelic.* Tearing my eyes away, I escape her thrall to shower off the dirt and blood clinging to me. I don't mind dirtying my sweet wife, but with sex and filthy words whispered in her ear, not the blood of other men.

The hot water washes over my body, and I lean against the tile for a moment, letting it carry away the evening's activities, before scrubbing at my skin and hair. Steam rises in the air, and my eyes half-close from exhaustion. My movements become robotic. Automatic. Until I finally crawl into bed and curl an arm around Eden's waist.

Sleep hovers around the edges of my consciousness when she twists around and blinks awake with an adorable yawn. "Where have you been? Did you just get home?"

"Yeah, Jonah and Hugo found shipping containers where Fabian was transferring women. It took some time and help from Dmitri and Blackthorn, but we rescued all the women at the docks. Thanks to you." I press a kiss to her forehead.

Her eyes widen in shock, though she shakes her head in disagreement. "I didn't do much. You and your brothers are the ones who actually saved them."

"If it wasn't for your gut instinct and the memory of that bracelet, we wouldn't have known to even look for those women," I say, recalling her concerns and the subsequent conversation I had with Rafe and the rest of the guys. Rafe immediately went into research mode, and it hadn't taken long for him to find some questionable correspondence and bank statements between Fabian and his clients.

Eden hums in her throat noncommittally as her finger draws a random pattern on my arm. "I know the internet can be a dark place, but I still can't believe those ASMR videos popped into my feed. That they led to this."

"Fabian is smart, but he's not clever enough to figure out that all the apps access IP addresses and tailor videos to users' local surroundings. He thought hiding his tracks in innocuous-seeming massage videos and vague hashtags would be enough. But it only takes one person with a bad feeling and computer skills to deep dive and discover what he's really up to. That's you and Rafe."

Eden nods thoughtfully before another yawn takes over.

"That's enough for tonight. You're still tired, and I've been up for hours. We can both use more sleep."

"You more than me after what you've had to deal with." She stretches to press a kiss to my collarbone then sighs. "Thank you for believing in me."

"Always," I murmur as we both drift off, our breaths evening out, our hearts beating together in a steady rhythm.

In sync.

As one.

CHAPTER TWENTY-FOUR

EDEN

"Sorry for the chaos." Jessie, the director at Polina's Place, brushes her bangs to the side and offers an apologetic smile. Clothes litter the furniture like a tornado whipped through the living room of the remote farmhouse, when in reality it was two dozen rescued women who raided the much-needed clean tops and bottoms.

"Don't worry about it. We can help organize everything again. That's why we're here," I say after folding a tee and starting a stack in a clear place on the coffee table.

When I arrived at the manor after work—where Corey and my boss still pester me about my whirlwind marriage and the temporary hire sent to fill in during my long absence—I caught Allie on her way to Polina's Place, and she asked if I'd like to join her.

After learning how many women Blackthorn rescued and sent to Polina's Place, I couldn't refuse the opportunity. They had to split the sizable group of survivors between two locations—the charity's main hub in downtown Boston at a secure monolith and this cozy farm out in the country.

Well, mostly cozy...

A shadow crosses the living room window. Another Blackthorn soldier on sentry duty.

Jessie sighs and adjusts the curtains to hide the obvious bodyguard. "Nathaniel filled me in on why we need beefed up security, but do they have to dress like the Terminator and stick so close to the house? We're surrounded by acres of land. Surely, they can catch bad guys before they make it this far."

"I told Mathias and Dmitri that they need more women in Blackthorn. At least enough for Polina's Place." Allie joins me in sorting the clothing as she eyes the now-covered window. "Guys with guns may be necessary for protection, but they're not exactly a welcome sight for most of the residents who pass through here, since a lot of them are escaping abusive partners."

"I told Nathaniel the same thing." Jessie rolls her eyes at the mention of one of Blackthorn's team leaders. Apparently, he's Dmitri's right-hand man and who the rest of the Blackchapel Bastards call on when they require personal security for sketchy situations.

Like what happened to Allie in Paris.

She told me all about Mathias's showdown with his father and how it ended in bloodshed. I pray it doesn't come to that with Luca and Enzo, but it's probably a fruitless endeavor. Revenge rarely involves peace.

Especially since Luca was the target of the drive-by shooting that brought Allie and Mathias together. One orchestrated by his father and carried out by D'Amora men.

"Oh..." A quiet voice comes from the hall. "S-Sorry for interrupting, but one of the girls started her period. She bled through her pants and needs replacements."

Jessie immediately goes to the timid woman with a gentle smile. "Of course. We're just cleaning up. This is Allie and Eden, and I'm Jessie, in case you forgot."

"Rowan."

"Such a pretty name. Now, what size are we searching for?"

She rattles off the size then hunches back into herself, a waterfall of red hair spilling forward to cover her face. An oversized hoodie skims her chest and belly while black leggings cover her legs. She fidgets, shifting on the balls of her feet, like at any moment she might need to bolt from the room.

Empathy clamps around my heart. I can't imagine the hell she's been through, and despite being safe here, it's still an unknown place with strangers roaming about.

"Do you need anything else?" Jessie asks after handing over a pair of blue jeans.

"No, t-thank you." Rowan escapes down the hall, and Jessie sighs.

"This is the toughest part: earning trust and proving you're not going to hurt them."

Allie pats her shoulder. "I know it's hard, but you've got this. I've been volunteering here long enough to know that you'll do the best you can for these women. It just takes time."

Jessie smiles in gratitude, and I vow to make volunteering more of a priority. I've been so focused on changing my life and dealing with my problems that I forgot there's a whole world out there that doesn't revolve around me.

Around *The Family*.

These women deserve the best care possible, and if I can contribute even a little bit to improve their situations then it'll be worth it.

***

The minute Allie and I return to Blackchapel three hours later, a Blackthorn guard is waiting on the stone steps leading inside and asks me to follow him at Luca's request. He leads me through barren hedges and gravel paths until we reach an enclosure covered in dormant vines.

Luca stands at its entry—a cute sage green door that probably hides well when everything is in full bloom.

"Thank you, Kenneth," Luca says as the guard retreats to give us privacy. He reaches out to take my hand and pull me closer for a kiss to the forehead. "How was your time at Polina's Place?"

"Good. We made decent progress in the wardrobe organization, and Jessie was able to inventory what was left and what she needs to restock." I study the tall brick wall that blocks anyone from seeing inside its depths. "What is this place? Allie mentioned a chapel being on the premises, but this doesn't look like a normal building."

"Because it's not." Luca unlocks the door with an old-fashioned key with elaborate loops and notches. It's a piece of whimsy in his roughened hand. "The chapel is on the east side of the manor and was here long before any of us arrived. This is something I added to the property years ago."

The door swings open, and he waves me through the arched doorway before closing us in with a soft click. A swing hangs from a thick tree branch while a bench rests in front of a cute pond surrounded by sleeping flowers. I can only imagine how magical it looks in the spring and summer.

"It doesn't look like much now due to the season, but this is a secret garden I built for my *mamma*," he explains with a barely detectable catch in his lowered voice. "When I first came to Blackchapel Manor, it reminded me of her favorite book,

The Secret Garden. Of course, the ensuing years of violence at Conrad's behest ruined that false belief, but after Dmitri and Aleksei created Polina's Place in honor of their mother, I wanted to do something similar to honor my *mamma's* memory."

"That's beautiful. I'm sure she would have loved this."

"It's not complete yet." His fingers break off a couple of random twigs from a bush. "I keep adding more to the garden whenever I find something that reminds me of her."

My eye catches on a familiar design. "Those butterflies look like the suncatcher you gave me," I point out. Rather than the delicate piece I have, though, these are sturdier to withstand the weather. Welded to the stop of iron stakes they decorate the garden at random intervals.

"That's because the same designer custom made them for me." Luca clears his throat, and I swear I see the beginnings of a blush on his cheeks. He scratches the back of his head with a sheepish shrug. "I wanted to incorporate a little bit of you into the space, too."

Tears well in my eyes as I stare at the sky, willing them away. Luca's incredibly sweet gesture settles in my chest and makes it harder to breathe. He wanted me in this memorial to his mom. A testament to the two most important women in his life.

"Has anyone else been here? Your brothers?" I ask, trying to move past the overwhelming blanket of vulnerability encapsulating both of us.

"No, just me. And now you. They know it's a private spot."

Crossing over to him, I twine my arms around his waist and raise on my tiptoes to land a gentle kiss on his lips. "Thank you for sharing this with me. I know it means a lot to you."

"It does," he agrees, dipping his head for a second kiss. "But you mean everything."

And there goes my heart.

CHAPTER TWENTY-FIVE

LUCA

"We've got a problem." Mathias walks into my office at Blackchapel Inc.'s headquarters unannounced. As COO, my workload has always been never-ending, but with time off for the honeymoon and how much time I spent at the manor after Eden's kidnapping, the piles of folders that needed my attention have become a mountain on my desk.

"What is it this time?" I ask exasperatedly. I'm not really in the mood to deal with another disaster. After the rescue mission on the docks and settling the women at Polina's Place, it's been blessedly quiet. Eden and I are growing closer each day and falling into a comfortable routine where she works at the daycare, I head to Blackchapel Incorporated, then we discuss our days over dinner.

It's domestic and perfect.

"There was a fire at our Huron warehouse. Took out the entire building. The security guards were able to get to safety, but the fire department couldn't put the flames out soon enough to save anything. Based on preliminary reports, it was arson. The fire burned hot and fast—a telltale sign of an accelerant."

"Shit." We are a billion-dollar company, so one warehouse loss won't break us, but it's not the money that concerns me. It's the act of war committed on our property. "Did Jonah check the security cameras for the perps? Did the guards see anything?"

"All we've got are two men in ski masks. They could be anybody." Mathias levels a look my way. "But an educated guess says they're Fabian's goons. Probably retaliation for saving those women."

"Did he think we were keeping the women held there?"

"A little recon would have disabused him of that notion," he says. "And why kill the women in a fire when stealing them back would be more profitable? I think he just wanted to fuck with us."

"Bastard," I mutter, aggressively shuffling a few folders into a neat stack to give my hands something to do other than punching a hole in the wall and wishing it was Fabian's face.

"Agreed... Insurance will cover the fire, but we need to figure out what to do with your half-brother and dad. Do you think he knows what Fabian's been up to? Maybe we can drive a wedge between the two of them." Always the planner, Mathias stares out the window overlooking the city as he considers our next course of action.

"Eden and I are having dinner with both of our families together for the first time tomorrow night. I'll try to suss out how much he's aware of."

"Dinner with the in-laws." Mathias grins. "Sounds fun."

Sounds like a minefield waiting to be triggered.

Eden isn't thrilled about the prospect of seeing Fabian, but as a mafia princess, she knows how the game is played. We have to remain composed until the time comes to strike.

CHAPTER TWENTY-SIX

EDEN

The D'Amora stronghold looms ahead, stately and majestic in its historical splendor. Guards buzzed our car through the iron gates, and I see my parents have already arrived for this official melding of our two families: Marino and D'Amora.

"Nervous?" Luca squeezes my hand gently as our driver pulls into the circular drive.

"A little."

"There's nothing to worry about. If Fabian tries anything, my fist will put him on the ground a second later."

"It's not Fabian I'm worried about," I admit. I trust Luca to protect me. Plus, there's no way Fabian tries something in front of his father, the don. He's too cowardly for such a blatant show of contempt—at least, that's my take on the man since we've never actually spoken. "It's my parents. I'm not sure what to expect from them."

"What do you mean? They'll be happy to see their daughter and tolerant of their new son-in-law. That's basic family dynamics, I believe, even for people who aren't part of the Boston mafia."

"Haha, very funny." I roll my eyes at his obvious amusement.

House staff welcome us into the spacious foyer then guide Luca and I into a sitting room reeking of wealth with its crystal chandelier and golden-flecked wallpaper. Leather sofas face each other in front of a massive fireplace where a painted portrait of Enzo, his wife, and a younger Fabian presides.

"Luca! Eden! The guests of honor have arrived." Don D'Amora barges forward with a wide grin and open arms as if we're beloved family instead of pawns in his political game.

Or is it Luca's game?

Mom and Dad stand from their stiff positions on one of the sofas and greet us with strained smiles. "How was Italy, dear?" my mom asks after a perfunctory hug.

"Beautiful. Warm." Turning to Enzo, I tilt my head downward in deference. "Thank you for gifting us your villa."

"Of course. That's what family is for. Speaking of... Fabian! Come say hello to your brother and his bride."

Luca's grip on my hand tightens before he sweeps a thumb over mine in a small gesture of comfort.

Fabian saunters closer and studies our held hands with a smirk. "Ah, the lovebirds. Tell me, *brother*, how is it fucking my ex-fiancée?"

Mom chokes on a gasp, the only sound in the aftermath of the bomb Fabian just dropped on our friendly family dinner. Silence reigns for another moment while my grip on Luca's hand tightens until my fingers start tingling from blood loss.

A growl emanates from his chest, like a beast about to pounce on his prey, but I'm not letting the evening devolve into bloodshed.

Enzo smacks his youngest son's head with a harsh blow. "Show some respect to your brother and his wife, or I'll have Ricci teach you how to behave." The reference to the D'Amora enforcer has my eyebrows winging skyward. It's no secret that whenever Enzo needs somebody taken care of—intimidated, injured, *or worse*—he calls Benito Ricci.

"Sorry, Father," Fabian murmurs under his breath, a death glare burning in his narrowed gaze. The apology is half-assed and an obvious lie, but it's enough to allow my mother to sweep forward and direct us to the dining room, expertly ignoring the tension among the D'Amoras.

You're a D'Amora, too.

The realization rattles my foundation just like it did the first time I learned of my impending nuptials. From the edges of the mafia straight to the red-hot center of danger and mistrust.

"Are you okay? We can leave if you want to," Luca whispers in my ear.

I shake my head and force a wobbly smile. "I'm fine. We expected trouble tonight, and Fabian didn't disappoint. Let him air his ire with an audience. It's safer to let your father deal with him than you taking matters into your own hands."

Luca grunts in disagreement but doesn't press the issue. I pray he keeps his composure the rest of the evening, too.

Only a few more hours to go.

We can make it.

***

Barely.

We barely made it through the entire evening without incident. It helped that Fabian left in the middle of the meal, citing some work call. Enzo hadn't looked pleased.

Things got awkward one more time when Enzo brought up Blackthorn, and my parents realized I was a pawn in the groom switch. But otherwise, my mom kept the conversation going with breezy updates about various families.

"A reward for your strength tonight at dinner." Luca presents a black velvet box, and my brows wing up in confusion as I shake off the memory of the evening. We just got back home, and I'm dying to strip and change into comfier clothes.

Another gift from Luca is unexpected.

"We're already married..." I say, cautiously accepting the box.

Luca grins. "It's not a ring, Butterfly. Just open it."

I flip the case open to find two gold figure-eight metal pieces with butterflies hanging from the bottoms. "Um, what are they?" They're missing studs to delineate them as earrings. Maybe they're charms? But where's the chain necklace or bracelet to accompany them?

"Nipple clamps. Of a sort."

"W-What?" Shock stiffens my shoulders as I study the pieces with new intensity. I wouldn't call our lovemaking vanilla per se, but this is definitely a new development.

"How..." I clear my throat. "How do they work?"

"Shall I demonstrate?" A wicked grin suffuses his cheeks. "Strip, Butterfly, and I'll show you."

Blushing, I wiggle out of the dress I wore to dinner then unclip my lavender bra, which leaves me in matching silk panties. Luca reaches a finger out and traces a nipple that immediately stands at attention.

Removing one of the clamps from its velvet bed, he slides it over my nipple. The cool metal is quickly warmed by his fingers. "By pushing the eight together, I can control how tightly it clamps together." He tests the binding, and I gasp at the sensation. "Instead of traditional clamps, these make it look like your nipples are pierced which is fucking sexy as hell."

"And as close as I'm ever going to get to pierced nipples." I shiver at the thought of needles so close to such a sensitive area.

"Trust me, I get it." He glances up at me with a sheepish expression before pulling his collar aside to reveal the small cross on his chest. I noticed all of the Blackchapel Bastards have the same design somewhere on their person. "The guys like to make fun of me, but I'm afraid of needles. It's why I only have this tattoo as part of our brotherly bond. It was pure torture sitting through the session."

I trace the black cross. "I'm happy to hear you've got at least one weakness."

Luca's confidence overwhelms me sometimes; it makes me second guess myself because I feel so inadequate when it comes to basic things.

Thanks Mom and Dad for such a strict and sheltered childhood growing up.

"I've got more than one, baby." He adds the second clamp to my other nipple before licking the tip. "Fuck, you're gorgeous. I'm going to fuck these tits and send these little butterflies flying."

"I'm not opposed to the idea," I whisper, willing to lay back and let him do it right now.

"My sweet, dirty girl. Always so willing to please me." He eases my panties down my trembling legs then guides me backward to sit on the end of our bed. Kneeling on the rug, his hands grab my knees and spread my thighs apart. "But first let me eat. I'm hungry for dessert."

His head dips to kiss along my inner thigh. Hot breath sends goosebumps raising along my skin, and I arch my back at the sensation, inhaling sharply.

Luca is too good at this. Attentive. Creative. And he only craves me. A miracle I still struggle to wrap my mind around.

My entire life I've considered myself average. Nothing special. No one has ever disabused me of that belief either.

Except for Luca.

I sigh as the wet tip of his tongue finds my clit and circles the aching button. My nipples swell with the pressure from the clips and the sweet tension he's building in my pussy.

"Luca..." My head falls back. My eyes close. My focus narrows to Luca and his talented mouth.

"Mmm, *carissima*." Luca's teeth graze my clit, and I jerk at the slight sting. "My little Butterfly is so pretty when her cunt's being eaten by her husband."

Two thick fingers fill my empty channel and rub the spongy spot with a direct line to my clit. Crying out, an orgasm suddenly rises and crashes, and Luca's growl of approval has more arousal seeping from me to coat his tongue and hand.

"Delicious." Luca lifts his head high enough to suck on my engorged nipples before he rips off his shirt and pants. One hand falls to his cock and strokes the hard length. "Scoot a little further down, baby, so I can slide between those pretty tits."

I immediately follow his instructions then cup my breasts to form a deep valley for his cock. The butterflies swing across my flesh in an erotic dance, and my breathing quickens at the sensation. It's like he didn't just lick me to completion a minute ago; my body is primed for more.

Luca climbs onto the bed and rubs the shiny head of his cock through the shadowy vee my breasts create. Precum slicks my skin, helping to ease the glide of his first slow thrust.

We both groan at the obscene picture his dark, throbbing cock makes against my pale breasts. I lick my lips and accidently lap at the purplish head, too.

"Fuck!" Luca shouts, jerking back for a second before plunging forward again.

This time I'm prepared and wrap my lips around the fat tip and suck until he shifts back. We continue this rhythm—Luca fucking my tits with increasing power, fulfilling his promise to make the butterflies on my nipples fly, while I suck and lick the sensitive head of his cock at the end of each thrust.

"How are you feeling, baby?" His raspy voice zings straight to my clit where he reaches back to test how wet I am, slamming his fingers into my rippling pussy.

"G-Good," I whimper, desperate to satisfy him. Desperate to experience another explosive orgasm.

"Prepare to feel even better." That's the only warning he gives before he removes the clamps and blood rushes back into my nipples.

I mewl at the sharp tingling feeling. It's multiplied when Luca stops thrusting between my breasts, so his teeth can capture a sensitive tip and flick it with his tongue.

"Luca, stop teasing me." More arousal coats my thighs, and I know the bedding is soaked beneath us. I need him stretching me full. I'm mindless with desire.

"Does my wife need my cock? Do you need to be fucked by your husband?"

God, I love when he talks dirty to me. It's crude and raw and makes me hot as hell.

"*Yes.*"

The next thing I know, his cock is buried deep in my pussy as Luca starts a punishing pace. Pounding hard with each thrust and sending me sliding up the mattress.

My hands catch on the headboard as I brace for each powerful impact of our joining. Luca may be sweet and gentle outside the bedroom, but inside?

He's brutal. A conquering warrior determined to claim his pleasure as roughly as possible, and I love it.

It's not practiced or tempered to an acceptable level of passion. It's unruly. No-holds-barred. *Honest.*

"Baby, I can't wait any longer. I need you to come for me," Luca pants in my ear. He tweaks my sore nipple, and it's enough to send me over the edge again.

My body shudders beneath him as he lets go. A primal roar booms from his chest, sweat gleams on his muscles.

He's beautiful.

And he's mine.

CHAPTER TWENTY-SEVEN

LUCA

"Is this the new hangout spot?" Rafe asks as he plops onto one of the giant beanbag chairs throughout the room. The chairs aren't really full of beans, or else the cats would have a field day, but their shape and malleability are reminiscent of the childhood seats—just modernized for adults.

Beanie chases a toy mouse across the floor before pouncing on Rafe's shoe to chew on the laces instead. Allie's cat, Pretty Kitty, lounges on a hammock attached to the window, napping under the sunlight.

The two cats get along as well as expected after weeks sharing the customized cat jungle the room has been turned into. They mostly keep to themselves—Beanie, energetic and playful, while the older Pretty Kitty sleeps a lot—but sometimes they choose to curl up next to each other, which Allie and Eden *ooh* and *ahh* over while snapping pictures.

I was searching for Eden when I found her with Allie in the cat room, Mathias joined at her hip. Then Jonah wandered in with Hugo, and now Rafe has joined the party.

"It was..." Jonah pretends to get up and leave, while Rafe flips him off with a roll of his eyes.

"We just need Dmitri to show up, then we can call an official manor meeting." Ever the peacekeeper, Eden ignores their playful insults, distracting Beanie from Rafe's shoelaces with a beribboned string at the end of a long wand.

"Don't hold your breath. Dmitri prefers training with Blackthorn soldiers when he has free time." As if we haven't spent years of our lives training already under Conrad's iron thumb.

Allie rests her head on Mathias's shoulder, watching Eden and Beanie. "Better training than kidnapping. I think we've reached our quota in this house for kidnapped women," she jokes.

"I second that opinion." Eden pins me with an exasperated glance. "No more kidnapping."

All of us guys raise our hands in surrender.

"Unlike my criminally minded brothers," Rafe drawls, a roguish twinkle in his eyes, "I don't need to hold a woman captive to keep her in my bed. My unique... *skills* are enough to keep her satisfied."

The women make mock gagging expressions as Hugo leans over to wallop Rafe on the side of the head. Mathias and I nod in gratitude for the quick reprisal.

Rafe laughs and jumps into defending his ridiculous claims, but I tune out his ramblings, happy to relax in a rare moment of peace. Between Eden's beating, finding and rescuing those trafficked women, and dealing with my troublesome family, my life has been a nonstop series of unfortunate events.

The only bright spot has been marrying Eden and finally getting to call her *mine*.

So, an afternoon hanging out with my brothers and my girl, along with a few cats, is a nice change. Even if it means listening to Rafe brag about his sexual prowess.

Eden scoots closer to me and bumps my shoulder with hers. "Are they always like this? All I've witnessed are the stoic mercenaries. Reverting to teenage boys is... different. Funny. Not what I'd expect from a group known as the Blackchapel Bastards."

"Stick with me, baby, and you'll never lack for entertainment." I grin, shaking my head at my brothers' antics. "This is what we're like when we don't have death and destruction breathing down our necks."

Her eyes widen to round amber orbs. "Geez, Luca. You make it sound like a pack of bloodthirsty vampires are about to descend upon us at any given moment."

"Sometimes it feels that way."

Sympathy softens her expression. "You realize you don't have to follow through on your plans, right? People change, and what you craved at fifteen doesn't have to be the same at thirty-five. You don't have to live with targets on your backs."

Her quiet words sink into my bones as I study each of my brothers. Oblivious to the serious turn of our conversation.

I don't think any of us have considered veering from our chosen path.

It's always been known that our fathers would pay for their part in our shitty childhoods, and their criminal ties—The Syndicate—would crumble to nothing. There was never a question of walking away. Of letting things stand.

"We've come too far to stop now, *carissima*," I whisper, though for the first time in decades, she has me wondering how true that really is.

CHAPTER TWENTY-EIGHT

EDEN

My hand sweeps across the bed, and a frown forms as I search for Luca. Cool sheets meet my fingers rather than his muscular warmth. Sitting up, I squint into the darkness, foggy sleep replaced by curiosity.

Where is he?

After leaving in the middle of the night to save those trafficked women without telling me, Luca has been better about letting me know when he has to duck out of our bed for business—even if it's a brief whisper and kiss before I fall back to sleep again.

The small lamp on the nightstand flicks on with a flip of a switch, but the sudden illumination shows an empty room, not my missing husband lurking in the dark. I check my phone for any messages, but there's nothing from Luca.

Biting my lip, I consider my options. Go back to sleep and wait for his return, or try to find him. Knowing I'll toss and turn for hours worrying about him, I choose the latter.

The bedroom door opens silently as the grandfather clock downstairs signals the hour. Two low drones. 2:00 A.M. Shadows creep over the hallway and walls, creaks and groans create a spooky soundtrack while the old manor settles for the night.

Those original gothic imaginings from a few months ago play in my mind again.

"I swear if I see a ghost..." I mutter to myself while carefully following the dark wood staircase down to the ground level. Rugs and carpet runners cushion my steps as I peek into the study, game room, and kitchen.

No Luca.

Hearing the faint splash of water, I follow a back hallway deeper into the manor. This is where the professional gym setup is located, along with an indoor pool and hot tub. There's also an outdoor pool, tennis and basketball courts, and a guesthouse on the grounds.

All the amenities rich and reclusive men with avenging agendas need, I think with a flash of amusement.

Humidity hits me in the face the moment I step into the indoor pool atrium. With the chilly autumn weather outside a wall of windows, the gigantic pool is kept heated to combat the cold, and the immediate production of sweat on my skin attests to its strength. Shrugging out of the robe I donned to cover up my flimsy nightgown, the silky material tumbles into a puddle on a nearby table as my gaze traces the smooth movements disrupting the pool of aqua before me.

Sleek arms cut through the water as Luca swims laps. I've heard Mathias and Rafe tease him about being part fish since he swims so much, but this is the first time I've seen Luca's obsession in person.

Crossing my arms over my chest, I sit in one of the white loungers surrounding the pool and watch his controlled strokes in awe. He's mesmerizing, and it's no wonder swimming is his escape. The rhythmic slice and kick of his body is enough to lower my blood pressure as a mere observer.

"Eden?" Luca emerges at the end of the pool and slicks his wet hair out of his eyes. He crosses his arms on the concrete ledge and glances up at me. "Why aren't you sleeping upstairs, baby?"

I hungrily devour the handsome picture he makes. Wet and gleaming. Muscles flexing.

Athletes have never been my type. Too cocky. Too intimidating. But I can't help but admire Luca's swimmer's build. It's bulkier than the ideal but those shoulders? Broad. Strong. And all mine.

"I could ask you the same thing," I say, clearing my throat and discreetly swiping at my pool for any rogue spots of drool.

"Swimming calms my mind."

"And what was on your mind? Your half-brother? That warehouse fire I overheard Mathias and Jonah talking about? Your dad or my parents?" The list could go on, and I grimace at all the... *bullshit* we've dealt with lately.

No wonder he needs an outlet to relax.

"Actually, I was thinking about what you said earlier. About letting go of this plan for revenge," he admits.

"Really?"

He rests his chin on his forearms and grunts in confirmation. "Yeah... I'm not sure I would have been opened to the suggestion before meeting you. I want you safe, and our current trajectory doesn't lend itself toward peace. Then, there's my dad." He sighs, a far off look entering his blue eyes.

"What about him?" I leave the lounger and settle beside him on the concrete ledge, dangling my bare feet in the pool. Luca shifts to float between my spread legs and circles my waist with his wet arms. My thin nightgown is soaked, but I don't mind, running my fingers through his slicked back hair.

"I don't know." Another afflicted exhale. His shoulders tense, and automatically, I begin massaging the hard muscles. "His whole demeanor lately. Welcoming me back with open arms. Giving me a family heirloom of my mom's. I never would have expected him to keep those. It's like I get glimpses of my *Papà* before Conrad and The Syndicate. Before he abandoned me."

"And you're wondering if there's a relationship worth saving. If you can forgive him for the past?"

"I guess so." He's quiet for a moment. "Then I remember how he hired someone to kill me in Paris, and it all goes out the window. I mean what kind of game is he playing where he acts like I'm a beloved son but also secretly wants me dead?"

I understand his frustration. My parents aren't the most demonstrative of people, but at least I know they love me in their own way. They'd never hire people to kill me. Their top concern is always safety.

"This is going to sound crazy, but have you thought about asking Enzo about that drive-by in Paris? I mean it's an open secret between you guys how there's resentment towards him and The Syndicate. Maybe laying everything out on the table will help you both move forward."

"You want me to ask my dad why he tried to have me killed." A lopsided grin blinks up at me.

"I told you it would sound crazy, but we're not exactly living in your run-of-the-mill world. Maybe Enzo would appreciate you taking the lead to get answers."

"Maybe... Or he'll pull a gun on me right there once he realizes his long game is ruined."

"Always so optimistic," I say sarcastically.

"Don't you know me by now, Butterfly? I'm a ray of fucking sunshine."

A surge of laughter bounces off the walls before it's cut off by a yelp of surprise. Luca's grip on my body tightens as he pushes away from the wall and tumbles me into the water.

"Luca!" My hand slaps his chest as I splutter to the pool surface. We're on the deep end, which means my feet can't reach the bottom and I'm reliant on him to stay afloat.

"Sorry, I couldn't help it. You were too much of a temptation sitting there all pretty and too dry for my liking."

"That's because I didn't come for a swim. I came to get you to come back to bed," I grumble.

"In a minute. For now, I want to recreate our time in Italy, where we just floated together on the sea. No worries. Nothing but you and me."

My ire softens at the sentiment. Luca can be so romantic sometimes. When he's not being filthy as *fuck*.

Expelling a breath of resignation, I loosen my hold on him and let him do the work of keeping us above water. "Fine, but you might have to carry me up to our room. I could probably fall asleep like this."

Warm water. An even hotter man cradling me in his arms.

It's a recipe for relaxation.

"I've got you, baby." A kiss to my forehead. "I've got you."

CHAPTER TWENTY-NINE

LUCA

The restaurant's twinkling lights create a glow around my wife. Her blonde waves are organized in a complicated design on the back of her head with soft tendrils framing her cheeks, and the intimate lighting from above blankets her in gold.

With our inconspicuous beginning, I've been determined to woo her with date nights and orgasms. A slice of normal in an otherwise unconventional life. We've even spent a few Sundays with her parents at their house for dinner. They've thawed considerably since our first meeting, but I'm not sure we'll ever have a close relationship.

"Did you enjoy your meal, Butterfly?" I signal our waiter for the check after our dessert plates are cleared.

"You know I did," Eden says, sharing a private smile with me. Her moans of delight had been a highlight of the evening, leading to a secret game of light caresses under the table.

She likes to pretend I'm the bad influence in our relationship, but my wife has a naughty streak she only lets out for me.

My Butterfly spreads her wings with each new day.

Gently guiding her toward the exit with a palm to her lower back, we collect our jackets from the coat check and step out onto the sidewalk. I texted our driver that we were ready to go, and he pulls up to the curb as the valet waves goodbye.

Our driver ducks his head while opening the back door, and an itch forms on the back of my neck, but I dismiss it. There's no reason to be paranoid. The man is Blackthorn, one of our security detail.

"Everything alright?" Eden can always tell when something is on my mind, and I never imagined how comforting it'd feel to be known so well. My brothers are good at deciphering my moods, but it's not the same.

This is Eden.

This is *my wife*.

"Yes, it's fine." My hand cups her bare knee and squeezes. Her burgundy dress has tempted me all evening with its deep vee and peeks at her lush thighs.

Settling in the backseat, I inhale a slow and steady breath through my nose before releasing it through my mouth—reaching for the previous calm I felt at the restaurant. The drive home is thirty minutes without traffic, but this is Friday night in Boston, so cars line the road, keeping us from speeding toward evening plans involving my face buried in my wife's pussy.

When the driver takes a right turn instead of left, that gut warning reemerges. Stronger and unwilling to be sidelined again. "You were supposed to go left back there," I say, leaning forward.

"Change of plans, sir. You and your wife are expected at the D'Amora estate."

The fuck?

Eden straightens beside me, confusion clouding her eyes. "Your father?"

Brows knitting as my mind races to piece together the endgame here, I shake my head in bewilderment.

"If Enzo wants to see me, tell him to set up an appointment rather than playing games while I'm out with my wife." I'm regretting leaving my weapons at home. Sure, I could reach out and break the man's neck with no problem, but that would leave Eden and I at the mercy of a runaway vehicle. One going nearly sixty miles per hour as the driver picks up speed on the highway.

I'm not willing to risk our lives on such a slim chance of survival.

But once we reach Enzo's? We're screwed.

I'll only have my hands to protect Eden.

Reaching into my coat pocket, I withdraw my phone to text an SOS to my brothers, but the driver clucks his tongue and lifts a gun into view. The barrel points at my chest, never wavering despite us rapidly changing lanes.

"I wouldn't do that if I were you."

Growling, I drop the phone in my lap and glare at the man. Hat pulled low. A number tattoo on his neck. That's probably what I noticed was off when the car appeared at the restaurant.

The Blackthorn soldier who originally chauffeured us downtown didn't have a tattoo there. I wonder what happened to him. If this guy killed him before stealing his place in the driver's seat.

The D'Amora man grins to reveal a row of chipped teeth. He must have been someone's punching bag over the years, or maybe he reveled in getting his ass kicked no matter how many teeth got knocked loose or cracked. It's obvious he's enjoying his rush of power over us.

The signs overhead show we're headed toward Weston as downtown Boston morphs into suburbs then mansions surrounded by trees and iron gates. I recognize this route. Enzo has a colossal estate hidden in the dense forest, in addition to his Beacon Hill brownstone. If memory serves, Enzo also bought Fabian a property out here.

A tentative, pink-tipped hand slides over my thigh, but I keep my gaze forward. Our driver keeps a sharp eye on us through the rearview mirror, halting Eden's progress toward my cell. By the time her fingers manage to tilt the phone to hide its light, we're pulling into a winding concrete drive. Lights glow from inside the modern monstrosity of gray stucco slapped onto a flat rectangular frame.

"This isn't Enzo's house," I mutter under my breath.

It's Fabian's.

The bastard waits for our arrival on the front steps like it's a damn holiday. *Shit.* This isn't good. I haven't seen my asshole half-brother since the disastrous family dinner weeks ago. He's been keeping a low profile. No more warehouse fires or movement on the docks.

I've been grateful for the reprieve from official Blackchapel Bastards business, but it's obvious his brief retreat into hermithood was a guise as he geared up for something bigger.

Like capturing me and Eden alone and unarmed.

Un-fucking-prepared.

Eden's thumb hurries across my phone's screen then flips it back over to hide her discreet messaging. I'm not sure what she sent or to whom, but I pray it gets to the right people—namely, my brothers.

"Welcome, brother. *Sister*." Fabian winks as we exit the sedan amid a waiting formation of five guards. The driver disappears into the house with a sly smirk.

Eden shrinks into my side, and I hold her close, studying our surroundings for a way out of this mess. Extra guards patrol the perimeter, creating a wall of soldiers I'd have to take down while somehow keeping my wife safe beside me.

I'm good, but not *that* good.

The quantity of hired mercs beats the quality of my training, which stings.

"What are we doing here?" I ask, keeping my body slightly forward as a shield to protect Eden. It's my only safeguarding option at the moment, and it's not much.

"Well, since you were so interested in my business by the docks. I thought I'd give my favorite couple firsthand experience at what you fucked up." Fabian motions to the guards, and we trek inside the gaudy foyer.

We're shown to the basement where there's a setup similar to the ones in the ASMR videos Eden used to watch, and I brace for impact. A camera sits on a tripod aimed toward a raised flatbed with white sheets. Various bottles of oils and lotions line the counter on one wall, while mirrors form a reflective backdrop on another.

What the hell does he have planned?

"That little rescue mission cost me," Fabian drawls, rubbing his hands together like your stereotypical evil villain. He probably likens himself to one. A narcissistic mastermind who can't be defeated. "Those women were meant to go to some very eager buyers. They were disappointed that you robbed them of the opportunity to test the whores' massage skills for themselves.

You and the rest of those Blackchapel Bastards stuck your noses where they don't belong, and now you and your little wife are going to pay."

So, that's what this is about.

It was a toss-up between me stealing his bride or those trafficked women.

After digging deeper, Rafe had figured out how the seemingly innocuous videos were basically sales pitches with unique hashtags and code words to alert potential buyers of each woman's price. It was a disgusting twist to something Eden had previously found comforting, and she hasn't watched an ASMR video in weeks since learning the truth about some of the videos.

"Time to recoup what you stole. You're going to fuck your chubby little wife on camera, then I'm going to sell her to the highest bidder before finally killing you."

"That's not going to happen," I warn. My arm moves in front of Eden to gently scoot her behind me.

Fabian gestures to the men blocking the two basement exits—an exterior door and the staircase we came down—and every single hired thug pulls out a gun and turns it toward us. "Strip and fuck, or else I'll do it. After all, your *Butterfly* was supposed to be mine in the first place."

There's a swift intake of breath from Eden as I contemplate our options.

Unfortunately, we have none.

Reading the seriousness in Fabian's gaze, I twist to whisper in Eden's ear while keeping the threat in front of us in view. "We'll be okay. Mathias and the guys will figure out something is wrong. I won't let anything happen to you, but we have to play along for now, okay?"

She nods shakily. Fear clouds her amber eyes, but she doesn't let the tears I see welling around her lashes fall. I know she doesn't consider herself particularly courageous after living the majority of her life sheltered by her parents, but I know the truth.

Eden is strong and courageous as fuck.

My hand soothes down her trembling spine. "Good girl," I praise softly.

"Save it for the video, brother." Fabian laughs. The rest of his men join in. All that's missing are buckets of popcorn to complete the distorted scene of a crowd settling in for an entertaining movie.

And Eden and I are in the starring roles.

Sitting on a rolling metal stool, I maneuver Eden so her back is to the camera and gently press on her shoulders, indicating she should kneel. She quietly follows the instruction, staring up at me with trust shining in her pretty eyes.

My fingers caress her cheek before I order, "Take out my cock, baby."

I'm facing the group of men around us with Eden between my spread thighs. I don't give a fuck who sees me, but no one will see my wife's gorgeous curves, so this is the best I can do on the fly—having Eden suck me off in front of our rapt audience.

It's a good thing I'm always hard around my wife or else we'd really have a problem. The wayward thought is a wisp of refreshing levity before it disappears in the face of reality.

Eden takes a deep breath, and I gently stroke a tendril of hair off her cheek, silently encouraging her to be brave for me. With a slow exhale, her lashes flutter closed as her pouty lips circle the tip of my cock. Someone groans in the background, but I block out the sound.

Her cheeks hollow as she slowly bobs up and down my thick length, drawing out my pleasure and giving my brothers enough time to swoop in and save the day. The men around us shift, lust permeating the air, and every ounce of my control is commissioned to focus on Eden. To stop from gagging in awareness of their disgusting desire.

At least Eden isn't gagging.

These bastards would love to see and hear that.

But she's being careful not to swallow me too far, though those tears she held at bay earlier are now spilling down her flushed cheeks. I tenderly caress the salty trails with my fingertips. Silently conveying my encouragement.

Fabian leans against the wall with a sneer. Flicking an imaginary piece of lint off his shoulder, he continues lounging to our left like it's an everyday occurrence for him to watch forced sexual interactions. Hell, it probably is with his latest line of work.

"I should have known it would come to this, brother. Hired help is useful, but when you need something done right, it's best to do it yourself." He waves his gun nonchalantly in the air like it's a damn king's scepter rather than a deadly weapon. "Those men in Paris. The team you destroyed at the docks. Two chances to finally put you down, and they failed. You won't be so lucky to escape a bullet a third time."

"Paris? You're the one who put out the hit on me? Not Enzo?"

Eden pauses her ministrations as I jerk in surprise. Her nails dig into my thighs, a mute hint to temper my reaction.

Fabian's smug admission sheds new light on the drive-by shooting. It makes more sense that my psycho half-brother wanted me dead versus our father who's been trying to integrate me back into the family.

"Our father? Kill his golden boy?" Fabian scoffs and stomps forward. "He's too weak to do what must be done to secure *The Family's* best interests. We can't have a bastard becoming the next don."

"That's what this is about? Inheriting leadership of the Boston mafia? Enzo isn't naming me his heir. It's going to be you." It's what Fabian was raised to do. While our father taught him the inner workings of the mob, his buddy Conrad was teaching me how to murder then dispose of an enemy.

It was never Enzo's plan to seat me at the top of *The Family* pyramid.

"That may be what his will says now, but it's only a matter of time before he changes his mind. He's already tied you to us with this sham marriage to a Marino. He's paving the way for you, and I won't have it. I will be the next don. Me!"

A crazed wildness transforms Fabian's expression, and dread creeps down my spine. Trapped animals are dangerous and unpredictable, and that's exactly what Fabian reminds me of right now.

This was already a shit situation, but a part of me had hoped to reason with Fabian. To rely on his desire for approval from Enzo—who would be furious about mine and Eden's kidnapping.

But Fabian doesn't give a fuck about what Enzo thinks. He's basically staging a preemptive coup.

Which means Eden and I are in major trouble.

CHAPTER THIRTY

EDEN

Last year, I watched a holiday movie where the heroine had to learn how to send covert texts. Her phone would be in her pocket, and she'd have to slip her hand into the hidden space and text her partner—the handsome spy training her to be his accomplice.

At the time, I thought it was funny and cute. I never thought I'd have to do something similar a year later, but that's exactly what happened the moment Luca's phone was in my grasp in the car.

Brief glimpses of his contacts appeared before I tilted the phone, so our driver couldn't see the screen's telltale light, then my thumb slid across the glass to form one word. *Fabian.* I hit SEND and prayed one of his brothers would be able to decipher the message's meaning.

What if I sent gibberish?

Everyone knows about phones' tendencies to autocorrect. Plus, my hand was none too steady since a gun was pointed our way.

It's too late to worry now.

Especially since both of our cells were confiscated the moment we stepped into the fake spa in the basement. In another life, I might think this is an excellent use of the extensive, white space. A relaxing oasis from life's stresses. Unfortunately, this is reality. One dominated by the mafia feud between two brothers.

I swear Fabian is trying to destroy every stress relief tactic I know. First, essential oils like eucalyptus. Then, those ASMR videos. And now spas.

Luca's palm cups the back of my head as Fabian rants about their father and his preference for his eldest son. My jaw aches from being kept so wide for so long, but I don't dare release Luca. I don't want to push Fabian into the next phase of his plan.

"You're doing so well, *carissima*." His low tone forms a comforting bubble around me, settling some of my nerves. He's talking about more than my blowjob skills, because it's a miracle I'm not hyperventilating.

After being kidnapped.

Again.

The only silver lining this time is Luca's presence. But we're still screwed. *Literally.* Because Fabian, the sick bastard, wants us to film a porno before shipping me off to another twisted pervert who purchases women against their will.

Bile rises in the back of my throat.

I'm going to throw up.

No, you can't.

I can't. I can't. I can't.

God, I should've stuck to my old mantra. My life might have been boring, but I'd been safe.

And alone.

Would you really want to trade away the moments you've had with Luca?

My mind doesn't have time to formulate a reply before the door atop the staircase crashes open, causing me to lurch backward with a choking cough, leaving Luca's wet cock to bob in the air. "What's the meaning of this? What the hell are you doing, Fabian?" Enzo's booming voice reverberates through the room. He and three soldiers file down the steps and process the scene before them. Considering Fabian's feelings toward his father, I'm not sure if Enzo's arrival is a good or bad thing, but at least it's taken Fabian's attention off us.

Luca tucks himself back into his slacks and helps me to my feet, sliding me protectively behind his hulking frame. I swipe at my swollen lips and swallow the lump of terror in my throat. Enzo and three men versus Fabian and his contingent of thugs aren't good odds.

"Ah, Father, nice of you to join us." Fabian pins a hateful glare on his dad as his men move to create a wall of weaponry between the two men. Thankfully, Luca and I are forgotten for the time being, something my husband seems keenly aware of as he slowly backs us to the opposite side of the room, the massage bed creating a measly barrier.

"I received an interesting call from Petrov. He thought there might be trouble between you and Luca. It looks like he was right."

Relief pours through me. Dmitri got my short message and sent Enzo to help. That must mean Blackthorn and the rest of the Blackchapel Bastards are on their way, too. We'll be saved as long as we stay alive long enough. A slim possibility with all the guns held aloft in the room.

"Of course, you decided to ride to the rescue for dear Luca, the prodigal son," Fabian snaps. "He's not the next don. I am. Your legitimate heir."

"Yet he's twice the man you'll ever be," Enzo counters.

Shoot... *Shit*. He should *not* be baiting Fabian. The man is already on edge.

"Fuck you!" The blast of a gun ignites a powder keg of violence as Enzo flinches then crumples from a bullet to his chest. A spray of red mists the air where he stood, and a scream explodes from my lips.

Strong hands haul me to the floor as Luca blankets me with his body. His sturdy frame crushes me to the marble tile. "Stay down, Butterfly. I'll die before I let something happen to you."

That's what I fear.

I don't want to lose Luca. I don't want him sacrificing himself for me. Because I love the overprotective man.

I love my husband.

Shouts of "FBI!" storm into focus, distracting me from the soul-deep realization.

FBI?

"FBI! Lower your weapons now!" A swat team sweeps into the room with raised rifles, followed by men and women in blue jackets with yellow block lettering. A couple of Fabian's men attempt to stand their ground but are quickly cut down. Fabian is one of the rebels, though it doesn't look like he got hit by a kill shot. He's rolling on the ground clutching his bleeding leg with a groan.

"We need an ambulance sent to..." An agent rattles out the house address as his colleague breaks from the group arresting the men still alive and approaches us.

"Special Agent Morris. Are you two okay? Do we need another ambo?"

Luca cautiously gets to his feet, and I gratefully accept his hand to stand on trembling legs. "No, I don't think so. Eden?"

"I'm fine. What happened?"

The FBI agent glances between us, the swath of dead bodies, and handcuffed criminals. "We've been investigating the D'Amora organization for years, but a random tip about a local trafficking ring put us on Fabian's trail. Our informant said something was going down today, so we were already preparing to storm the castle, so to speak. When you two showed up, then Enzo, we knew it was time to act."

"Thank god you did." I exhale a relieved sigh. And thank god they took their random tip—probably sent by Rafe—seriously.

"We'll need your statements before you'll be free to go, but you can wait outside while we clean this up." Special Agent Morris gestures to the chaotic scene around us. The scent of blood and eucalyptus oil hangs in the air, and I breathe through my nose, the noxious fumes giving me a headache.

"Thanks, we could use the fresh air." Luca tips his chin in a *goodbye for now* then hustles me out the exterior basement door the FBI breached. Yellow caution tape already forms a barrier around the mansion, and red and blue strobe lights paint the surrounding trees in color.

I can only imagine the gossip this will churn up with the neighbors. Even though they're spread out, there's no hiding the flashing lights and loud sirens heading this way.

"Guess it's a good thing you plan on dismantling the Boston *Family* if the feds have been on their tail," I murmur, randomly latching onto that bit of news.

Luca tugs my coat sides tighter together as a shiver wracks my body, but I don't think it's the weather seeping through the wool cloth. I think shock may finally be settling in as my adrenaline wears off.

"The feds are always investigating potential mob ties. Who knows how close they were to anything concrete before Fabian decided to go rogue."

"Are the feds on to Blackthorn, you think?" The new worry compounds my already shot nerves.

"Not as far as I know, but we've got an inside man." Luca grins at the admission.

"Of course you do." Luca and his brothers are master planners. They don't go off half-cocked like Fabian did. According to Allie, Mathias is particularly anal about ensuring their safety and secrecy.

Once we're on the outskirts of the bustling mix of local cops and FBI agents, Luca faces me and cups my cheeks. "Are you sure you're okay? I could have lost you in there. And what he made us do. What *you* had to do—"

I place my finger over his lips to stop his guilt-ridden speech. "Like I told that special agent, I'm fine. Shaken up and indefinitely put off from ASMR massage videos, but fine. You protected me as best you could in there." Wrapping my arms around his waist, I hug him close, comforted by his warmth. The steady rhythm of his heart. Signs of his life—safe and unharmed. "What about you?"

He strokes the hair at the back of my head and presses a kiss to the tangled crown. My poor updo didn't survive the night. "I'm still processing everything, but I'm okay. Fabian won't bother us anymore with his upcoming prison sentence."

"True... But what about your dad? I saw them doing CPR on him. Do you think he's dead? That's a lot to deal with—your half-brother killing your father."

"We've only recently reconnected." He shrugs, though there's a tinge of something else in his voice. Forced nonchalance. Like he's trying to convince himself that he doesn't care what happens to Enzo. "It's not like I didn't plan my own act of revenge against him with my brothers. This just removes one more brick in The Syndicate foundation."

"Luca..." I drop my head back to meet his shuttered gaze. Powering through the sudden fatigue weighing on my limbs, I reiterate the points of our last conversation about his dad. "It's okay to change your mind. To love your dad. Or to not hate him as much as you used to. The two of you have spoken a lot recently, and he gave you those cufflinks from your mom..."

"I know. We'll see how—"

"Luca! Eden!" Mathias's powerful voice carries on the wind, and we turn to find the entire Blackchapel Bastards contingent, plus Allie, converging on us. How they got past the yellow police tape, I have no clue, but I'm thankful to see them. "What the hell happened? Dmitri texted us that he got a weird message from you, then Rafe tracked your phone here. Are you both alright?"

Stupid Fabian.

It didn't even occur to me that Rafe could track our phones. By the time he had his thugs confiscate them, it was probably too late to turn them off or destroy them before the signals bounced off the nearest cell towers.

I let Luca explain the events of the evening, preferring to sink quietly into his comforting embrace. All I want is to sleep for the next twenty-four hours, but first we need to talk to the FBI and relay our story a second time tonight.

It's bound to be hours before I'm cocooned in the safety of Blackchapel Manor and our cozy bed. Hours before I'm free to tell Luca the truth I realized earlier.

That I've fallen for my husband.

CHAPTER THIRTY-ONE

LUCA

The hospital is eerie at 3:00 A.M.

After giving our statements to the FBI, we were allowed to leave Fabian's cordoned property, but instead of going home, Eden insisted we follow Enzo to St. Anthony's where he was receiving emergency surgery.

Admittedly, I didn't fight her too much.

It's funny... I've been intent on revenge against my dad for decades, ever since he abandoned me at Blackchapel Manor after my mother died. But experiencing the threat of his actual death has shifted my perspective.

When I saw Enzo go down from Fabian's bullet, a slew of emotions bulldozed the walls I'd built. Cracked the ice-cold barrier I kept between us. Allowing good childhood memories I'd long forgotten to emerge.

As hungry as I am to bring down The Syndicate, I don't want to kill Enzo anymore. He's a cog in the giant machine, and maybe it makes me weak, but I can't have his death on my conscience.

I'm not sure I want to repair our relationship to what it could have been pre-Conrad and his murder lessons; I'm not sure that's even possible.

But I'm open to something... *more*. A compromise on what I've always planned.

Eden will probably rejoice at the news, especially since she's the one who planted the seed of reconciliation in the first place.

I pace empty hallways with Eden, who shadows my footsteps, too wired to rest in the waiting room with everyone else. My brain buzzes with how our date night turned into this dragged-out nightmare.

"I don't think you need any caffeine. You've got too much energy as it is," Eden says as she blocks me from putting a dollar in the crappy coffee vending machine.

Sighing, I nod and put the bill back into my wallet. "You're probably right."

She covers a yawn as we continue our trek around the sterile halls, the metallic smell of medical machines and cleaning products burning my nose. Every once in a while, a nurse will appear, but for the most part, we're left alone.

"I may not be tired, but you are," I say, noting the purplish shadows under her eyes. "Why don't you let Mathias and Allie take you home? Who knows how long I'll be here?"

"I'm not leaving you, Luca."

"Butterfly..."

"No, don't *Butterfly* me." She draws me into a darkened room with an empty bed and dormant machines. "I'm not leaving you. I... I had an epiphany tonight at Fabian's." Her head ducks down as a blush colors her round cheeks.

"An epiphany?" Shit, is she about to tell me she wants a divorce? That it's too dangerous being with me? I already knew that was true. After all, that's why I held off on claiming Eden for so long, but now that I've had her, I can't let her go.

I won't.

Even if that's what she wants.

I'll give my sweet wife anything... *except her freedom.*

She taps the toe of her shoe against the tile then peeks up at me. Nerves bounce in the air, zapping me with the possibility of her rejection.

Tonight was a lot. I had her get on her fucking knees to suck my cock in front of strangers and my half-brother. On film. *Which reminds me, I need to get a hold of that camera and erase the footage.*

"I love you," Eden blurts out, and I freeze at the unexpected declaration. "Oh my gosh, I'm sorry! I didn't mean for it to spill out like that. I—"

I steal a quick kiss from her rambling lips. Pleasure seeps into my bones. "You love me?"

"Um..." Confusion knits her brows as I claim another sip of her lips. "Yeah, I do. I know this isn't the most romantic place to tell you, but I need you to know I'm not going anywhere. You're stuck with—W-What are you doing?"

My foot knocks the door closed, so we're cloaked in privacy. "Kissing my wife. Who loves me." My hands sneak under her dress to squeeze her juicy ass as I grind my erection into the sweet heat between her thighs.

A bit of tension release sounds perfect right about now.

Especially when my woman just admitted to *loving* me.

"Luca... We can't have sex here. This is a hospital. Your father is in critical condition."

"That's not going to change whether we're haunting the halls or waiting in that room with everyone else or fucking right here, right now." I unbutton my slacks for the second time tonight and free my hard cock, notching it at the entrance of Eden's pussy. "We survived my crazy brother, an FBI raid, and you just told me you loved me. I'm not letting another moment pass without feeling you wrapped around me."

"I don't know," she wavers, her fingers digging into my shoulders as I circle her clit, preparing her for my swift entry.

"I love you, Eden. I've loved you for months. From afar when I watched you. From the end of that bed at Blackchapel Manor while you recovered from being beaten. You're my resilient little Butterfly, and nothing is going to change how I feel."

I seal the promise with a flex of my hips, sinking deep into her wet cunt. Eden gasps but doesn't push me away. Her body wants this, too, even if her mind is trying to catch up.

I've barely gotten started when a tear drips down the side of her cheek to dampen mine, and I immediately stop. "Fuck, did I hurt you?"

"No, these are happy tears. Because you love me, too." She shudders in my arms and wraps her legs around my waist as I pin her to the wall. Emergency exit posters have never looked so sexy as they do with my wife braced against them. "You *see* me. All my life I've been in the background. I've never been important to *The Family*, never been noticed. Until *you*. Why can you see me, Luca?"

"Because you're mine," I growl.

Eden whimpers, and the sound is enough consent to re-energize me. Our bodies push and pull with each labored breath. Love twining in the air to tie us closer together.

I spread hot kisses over her face and neck, down to the deep cleavage created by her heavy breasts. Eden scratches at my scalp, my shoulders, wherever she can reach as she covers me with the most beautiful three words in the English language.

I love you. I love you. I love you.

Together, we find release.

Together, we find peace.

Slowly, we come down from our high with soft sighs and nuzzling kisses, content to remain in this cozy bubble for a little while longer.

Except there's a loud bang on the door.

"Hey, lovebirds! The surgeon is waiting to give you an update. Wrap it up and get out here." Jonah must have been the lucky one elected to corral us back to reality.

"Fucking asshole," I mutter with no heat.

Giggling, Eden slides down my body and shuffles to the sink and counter to clean up the mess between her thighs. I'm about to stop her—the thought of my seed dripping down her legs, my scent covering her curvy little body intoxicating—but she spears me with a knowing stare, and I stay silent.

There will be plenty of times in the future when I can live out that particular fantasy.

We leave the room hand in hand minutes later to hear what the doctor has to say about my dad, and a pit forms in my stomach, despite the previous satisfaction I claimed from Eden's giving body.

"Your father has a long recovery ahead of him, but we're confident about his prognosis. Barring any complications, he should make a full recovery. If you'd like, you can sit with him." The doctor flips the cover over his tablet and the hospital's digital file for Enzo, which basically states how he's lucky to still be alive since Fabian's bullet nicked a lung.

"Thank you," I say, glancing down the hall to the post-op room they wheeled Enzo to. The doctor retreats to the nurses' station and hands over the tablet for charging. I share the good news with everyone in the waiting room then grab Eden's hand.

It's dim with beeping machine lights and what spills over from the overhead hallway fluorescents as Eden and I step into Enzo's private room.

His upper body rests at a reclined angle in the hospital bed, tubing and wires a complicated web leading from his supine body to the various medical devices monitoring his health. Oxygen fills his injured lungs from the nasal cannula. The wrinkles around his eyes and mouth are more pronounced, and for the first time, it hits me how fragile my father truly is.

He's always seemed larger than life with his commanding presence and air of authority, but looking at him now—a weathered man in his sixties—the signs of age are more obvious. The evidence of his mortality more alarming.

"Are you alright?" Eden whispers, compassion shining from her eyes. She tugs her hand free from mine to pat my chest.

Clearing my throat, I clench my jaw and nod. "Sorry. I didn't expect seeing him like this to affect me so much."

She rubs the spot over my pounding heart. "No need to apologize. He's your dad, despite the painful history between you two. It's natural for emotions to rise. You are human, after all," she lightly teases with a gentle pinch to my pec.

"Still... I didn't—"

"Luca? Is that you, son?" Enzo's graveled croak interrupts us, and I stride to his bedside, shocked to see him awake.

"Fighting the anesthesia? You should still be resting, Papà." It's been forever since I've called him by the more intimate paternal moniker, but somehow, it feels right.

"I heard your voice and had to know what happened." He struggles to sit more upright. Immediately, my arm braces against his back to help him while Eden rushes to fill a cup with water. Enzo accepts it with a trembling hand, and I keep a watchful eye on each slow sip from a straw.

"The FBI raided the place. Fabian is alive and in custody," I say. "You're lucky to be alive and out of surgery. The feds are focused on Fabian's operation, so *The Family* is safe for now. I contacted your underboss, Vinny, about shoring up security."

"Good, good." Enzo's eyes close for a moment before opening to pierce me with a proud stare. It's unsettling to notice how similar our coloring is. I've avoided our similarities for so long, wanting nothing of his, yet here's the proof that I'm his son.

"I always knew you'd make an excellent successor. Your no-good brother recognized it, too. I should have dealt with Fabian's reckless ways years ago, but I let misplaced fatherly love blind me to the level of hatred he harbored for the both of us."

"It doesn't matter now." I pat his shoulder, the frail bones beneath his hospital gown causing a wave of protectiveness to crash forward. *What the hell?* I may not want Enzo dead anymore, but it's difficult experiencing a complete one-eighty in my heart and mind.

This fucking night.

It's turned my entire world upside down.

"Excuse me." A nurse briskly enters the room to check his vitals. Her light blue scrubs swish matter-of-factly with every efficient step as Eden and I give her room to work. "Your father needs to rest now. You can visit again later."

Murmuring our goodbyes, we return to the hall and walk to the waiting room. My brothers and Allie sit in the uncomfortable plastic chairs, sharing matching curious expressions once they spot us. They're here to support me however I need, even if that means Enzo won't face the wrath of the Blackchapel Bastards.

I haven't mentioned it outright yet, but the fact that I'm in the hospital checking on Enzo's health is sign enough that the plans have changed.

"How is he? How are you doing?" Allie asks, the fondness in her eyes magnified by her glasses. She and Mathias stood to greet us the moment we entered the room.

Glancing around at my support system, a small smile of gratitude tugs at my mouth. "Enzo is tired but okay, and I'm good. I've got my family and the love of my life."

"And the entirety of the Boston mafia on your shoulders, I'm guessing," Mathias interjects as he gives me a hug. The rest of the guys follow.

"We might need to promote someone else to COO of Blackchapel Incorporated with my new responsibilities," I joke. Months ago, when Eden asked, I told her we'd disband my father's legacy, yet now I'm choosing to run the organization in his place until he recovers. Already barking orders to his underboss.

And after that? Who knows?

Maybe I *will* become the next D'Amora don.

I already have a queen fit to rule.

***

Love epilogues? Check out Eden and Luca's here[1]!

PROLOGUE

JONAH ANDERSON

ELEVEN YEARS OLD

"You bastard! You lying son of a bitch!" Mom shouts from the master bedroom of our penthouse on the Upper East Side of New York City. Dad arrived a half hour ago with a briefcase and a grim expression. He sent me to my room after handing over a small drone wrapped in shiny gold paper. The gesture is straight out of his *How to Buy My Son's Love & Allegiance* playbook.

He probably couldn't care less about my love, but a part of me still likes to believe my dad cares about me for more than just blind loyalty when he needs backup against Mom.

Gift given, Dad proceeded to the master suite where Mom always lazes the day away in her massive bed, feathered robe, and an unending supply of wine.

Their fighting began almost immediately once the door shut.

Which is never a good sign.

Throwing the drone on my bed, I tiptoe back into the hallway to eavesdrop. Not that I need to be stealthy. Mom and Dad are only ever aware of what's going on in their own little worlds.

"Susan is getting suspicious, and she's threatening to call her father to pull his funding. You know how important this campaign is, Pamela. This is the next step on my way to the presidency. Being named the state's next governor will cement my leadership abilities."

I roll my eyes. I've heard Dad's plan to become President of the United States so many times I could repeat it in my sleep. He's obsessed with holding the most powerful position in America. Power and prestige—two words that define Phillip Anderson. But it's hard to obtain those things without money and a squeaky-clean public image. Which is why he's here dumping my mom. We've been his dirty little secret for years. Something I found out last year after overhearing a conversation Dad was having with his best friend, Congressman Lieber.

Mom is his mistress, and I'm his bastard son.

If the public ever found out, he'd be *persona non grata*. That's what he said. I'd had to look up what it meant on the computer. And if his father-in-law ever found out that Phillip was cheating on his perfect princess? Well, that would be career suicide *and* a suspicious murder. Probably. I couldn't tell if Dad was serious when he mentioned *disappearing* and *fish food*.

"Fuck you, and fuck Susan!" There's a crash from the room, and I'm guessing Mom threw one of her wine bottles at Dad's head and missed. The splatter of red will match the rest of the splashes she's created over the years. At first, Dad ordered a maid to clean up the mess, then he just stopped caring. It's a twisted mural to their relationship.

"What am I supposed to do with your son when you're kicking us out of our home? The little devil is hell to raise already. How can I survive with the measly pittance you're offering?"

Uncomfortable with this turn of the conversation, my eyes scan the hall and snag on the open door to my bedroom. Posters of baseball players and trophies from my little league games litter the walls and shelves. It's the only home I've ever known, and Dad is making us leave?

Scooting closer to hear better, I place my ear on the wall.

"I've got plans for Jonah. I'm sending him to a sort of boarding school run by an old associate of mine. Conrad Steele has taken in a couple of other boys, so Jonah will fit right in."

Boarding school?

"And what about me?" Mom's tone has changed, softened to a whine. I imagine the pout on her Botoxed face. Time to switch from angry bitch to sniveling pet.

The unflattering description of my mom's manipulative personality matches her hateful feelings towards me. *Devil. Menace. Useless wretch.* There's no love lost between Mom and I. None between me and Dad either, if I'm being honest.

My parents aren't the loving type.

They're nothing like my teammates' parents.

That doesn't mean I want to be shipped from the only home I've ever known to a stranger's weird boarding school.

Sinking to the expensive runner lining the middle of the hall, I bang my head against the wall as Mom and Dad continue to fight. *What am I going to do?* My hands ball into fists as I blink back tears, erecting a steel barricade around my heart.

Mom and Dad won't break me.

Let them do what they want.

I'll survive.

After all, if I'm a devil, I'm meant to thrive in whatever hell I end up in.

***

Continue reading Jonah and Valerie's story in *Devil's Kiss*!

THANKS FOR READING & DON'T FORGET TO RATE/ REVIEW!

Please consider leaving a rating/review. Ratings & reviews are the #1 way to support an indie author like me.
The more reviews, the more my books are shown to other potential readers!
And they serve as guides to readers on whether or not to take a chance on an indie author.
I appreciate your support!
XO, Hallie

ABOUT THE AUTHOR

Hallie prefers steamy, insta-love stories where curvy girls are claimed by filthy-talking heroes. And when she ran out of reading material, she decided to write her own stories. If you want a quick, hot read, she's your girl!

Don't miss out on Hallie Bennett updates by joining her VIPs here[1]!

---

1. https://www.thearrowedheart.com/hallie-bennett